Books by
Jeremy Soldevilla

Thief Creek
Murder in the Mountains
Second Chances

BY JEREMY SOLDEVILLA

thief creek

Christopher Matthews Publishing

www.christophermatthewspub.com

Boston, Massachusetts

Thief Creek

Cover image: Jeremy Soldevilla
Cover Design: Armen Kojoyian

ISBN: 978-0-9833164-0-4
ebook ISBN: 978-0-9833164-5-9

Available from local and online bookstores
or order this book online at
www.christophermatthewspub.com

Christopher Matthews Publishing
Boston

Printed in USA

Acknowledgments

My thanks to Bozeman Police Detective David McManis for his technical advice; the Bozeman Ink Slingers—Sharon Dunn, Ellen Figura, Dennis Flath, Sue Geske, Frank Seitz, Kathy Tyers, Jamie Upschulte, Donna Wallace, Marci Whitehurst and Don Wolslagel; and especially my wife, Melissa, for giving me the freedom and encouragement to write.

ONE

Ed Loomis, the clerk at the Lewis and Clark Gas-N-Go in Lame Elk unlocked the front door and started the same old routine of opening the store he had performed for the last seven years. As if on autopilot, he flipped on the lights, turned off the alarm, made the coffee, hauled water out to the windshield washer buckets by the gas pumps, came back in, opened the cash register and counted the till just as he'd done every morning for years. Just another day.

He leaned across the counter and scanned the store. Gum wrappers on the floor. Magazines askew. Yesterday's papers unbundled and slipping from the bottom shelf to the floor. The wastebasket looked like it was having a bad hair day with trash and curlicues of register tape overflowing the top. He shook his head and sighed heavily. *Doesn't that night kid ever clean up before closing? Is it asking too much for him to do his job right? When I was in high school, I was glad to have a job, and I did what was expected of me. Didn't leave a mess for the next fella.* He shook his head and shrugged. *Oh well. It'll give me something to do. Mornings are so damn slow anyway.*

He shuffled to the supply room, grabbed the broom and swept down each aisle. Then he brushed the dirt and trash out the back door. He straightened the magazines, bundled yesterday's newspapers and cut the plastic strap on today's papers. He adjusted his glasses and glanced at the headlines. *Wonder what idiocy is going on out there.* "Out there"—so far away from Lame Elk—his dinky town hidden in the far northwestern corner of Montana. There was never anything important to report locally except maybe the annual Spring photo of a bear or moose that wandered into town.

The big headline today shouted, "TIGHT MONEY MAY MEAN NO TOWN FIREWORKS THIS YEAR." That would be just fine with him. He liked to get to bed early anyway. Didn't need to have all that noise disturbing his sleep. *Let the kids shoot off their firecrackers and blow their dang fingers off. What else is going on?*

He skimmed the other headlines—WESTERN GOVERNORS CONFERENCE IN HELENA; 3 ESCAPE DEER LODGE PRISON; GUN ACTIVISTS PROTEST IN GLACIER NATIONAL PARK. Now, that was something worth reading. *Government's always trying to take our guns away. Dang East Coast politicos. Over my dead body.* He speed read the article, mumbling the words to himself. When he finished, he dropped the newspaper back on the stack and then arranged the papers on the shelf.

Loomis headed behind the counter and bent to pick up the wastebasket when the bell on the front door tinkled. He glanced at the clock. 7:45. That would be Colton Anderson. Right on time.

"Mornin', Ed," the young deputy greeted him as he strode to the coffee machine and poured himself an extra-large cup. It still amazed Ed how scruffy little Colton Anderson had grown so tall and handsome. Probably the always crisp uniform made him better looking than he was, but still . . .

"Howdy, Colton. Whatcha got going on today? Passing out speeding tickets to the high school kids?"

Anderson took a healthy sip of the coffee and grimaced. "I ought to arrest you for false advertising. You call this stuff coffee? You drop a dirty sock in here or something?"

"Same free coffee you come in and drink every dang day. Quit your bellyachin'. You don't like it, take your business somewhere else."

"And where else would that be? You're the only place open in the morning."

"Well, I guess you're stuck then, aren't ya?" Loomis stuck his grizzled chin at the officer.

Anderson chuckled and picked up a newspaper and dropped it on the counter. He scanned the headlines as he fished two quarters out of his pocket. "Did you read this about the jail break in Deer Lodge last night? Says they haven't had a prison break for twenty years."

Ed craned his head, pushed his glasses up on his nose and peered at the article the deputy pointed at. "Nope. Didn't read it. That's all the way over to Deer Lodge. Ain't got nothin' to do with me. Boys are probably all the way to Mexico by now, drinking margaritas and eating burritos in some cantina. I did read about them gun protesters over in Glacier, though. They aren't going to be happy till we're all defenseless. I say, let 'em try. Dang East Coast tree-huggers. No one's taking our guns away."

He wanted to go on with his usual diatribe about gun control, but he could see Colton was engrossed in the newspaper and not paying attention. He swept up the fifty cents and rang it into the register.

"Hmmm," huffed Anderson as he finished the article and tucked the paper under his arm.

The old clerk wasn't in a hurry to see him go. Colton was likely to be his only customer all morning except for the one or two who might grab some gas out at the pumps, but they rarely came in the store anymore. He wouldn't have anyone to talk to but himself. "How's Jack Tate treating you?"

"The sheriff's cranky as ever. He's almost as crochety as you, Ed."

"Heck, Jack's been cranky since grade school. He's been good to you, though, huh?"

"I guess so." Anderson turned to leave. "Well, Ed, you have yourself a good day."

"I sure will. You too, Colton." Just before the deputy reached the door, Ed called out, "Oh, and Colton?"

Anderson stopped and waited but didn't turn around.

"You be careful out there." Ed cackled at his own joke. It was a line from his favorite cop show from back in the '80's, *Hill Street Blues*. He doubted Colton even knew the program, but it tickled him to say it every morning as the deputy headed out the door. As if there was anything to worry about on the "mean streets" of Lame Elk, Montana.

The deputy waved goodbye with the newspaper in the air and left the store. Ed was still chuckling when the tiny doorbell jingled as the door closed behind him.

Ed stuffed the overflow back into the wastebasket and carried it out to the dumpster in the back alley.

"Gol dang it!" he swore and slammed the wastebasket on the ground. The big metal lid to the dumpster was flipped up, and there was trash strewn all over the alley. The dang kid left the padlock off the dumpster last night, and a bear or a raccoon or some other critter must have gotten in there and had a field day with the garbage.

He walked around collecting trash and shoving it into the dumpster, cursing and mumbling to himself with every piece. From inside the store, he heard the bell on the door tinkle as someone entered. He threw one more crushed cardboard box into the container and slammed the lid down. He slipped the padlock into the latch and made a mental note to have the kid come out and clean up the rest of the mess when he got there after school.

Ed re-entered the store and let the screen door slam behind him. On the way to the register, he glanced over the counter and saw that four men had come in. No one he knew. They strolled the aisles, picking up this and that, so he tidied up the counter while they shopped. He stuck some fresh hot dogs onto the rollers in the heated display cabinet. Of course, the kid hadn't removed the old hot dog from the cabinet. He snagged the wrinkled wiener with the greasy tongs and threw it in the wastebasket and shook his head and sighed. He hung the tongs on their hook and took his place next to the register.

For the first time, he took notice of the four men in the store.

At first glance, Ed was glad to see customers. He liked to chat with folks; find out where they were from and what they were doing off the beaten track in Lame Elk. In the fall it was usually hunters. In the summer it might be campers or tourists winding their way back to Oregon or Seattle after visiting Glacier Park. Winter was just dead. If it wasn't for his old cronies stopping in to play cards in the long winter afternoons, they might just as well close up the store. Except then no one would have any place to get gas. This time of year, it would likely be fishermen, which would mean bait sales and maybe fishing licenses. With nothing better to do, he liked to play a game with himself, trying to figure out where people were from and what they were doing in his little town.

The closest of the four men stood with his back to the counter, searching through the bags of snacks on the end cap in front of him. The other three wandered around further up in the store, loading up with various items. *Take your time boys. We could use the sales.*

"Everything on that shelf there is 25% off," he said to the man's back.

The fellow turned his head and grunted, "What?"

Ed raised his voice. "I said everything on that shelf is twenty-five percent off. Nothing wrong with it, we're just trying to move the merchandise."

"Yeah, I can see the sign," the man grumbled, then turned back.

Just trying to help. No need to get snippy. Ed pushed his glasses up on his nose and squinted across the aisle, trying to get a closer look at the man. *I'll be damned, that ol' boy's missing an ear.* Sure enough, there was a gnarled stump where his left ear should have been. On closer inspection, the side of the man's face that he could see had a nasty scar running the length of his cheek from the ear stub to his chin. Bear attack? Car accident? *Dang, that had to have been a rough one, whatever it was. Wonder what his story is.*

His curiosity aroused, Ed scrunched his face and surveyed the three other men in the store. The fellow coming from the refrigerator section was huge. Maybe six foot four with tattoos covering both his arms. He had picked up two cases of Bud Lite and balanced them with one hand while he grabbed a family size bag of Doritos and stuck it between his teeth. There was something not right about his face. Squinting for a better look, Ed noticed an odd shape to the man's mouth. His lip was split clear up to his nose, exposing his top three teeth. A harelip. That's what they call that. He recalled that the Fisher boy was born with one of them.

The Doritos bag behind the one the huge guy had chosen fell to the floor. Rather than pick it up, he kicked it out of his way. The old man opened his mouth to tell the big lug to pick it up, but on second thought, said nothing.

A prickly feeling began to crawl up the back of Ed's neck. He didn't like the looks of these two. But, heck, they were buying a lot of stuff, and Lord knows the store could use the money. Still, it paid to be on your toes. Out in the boonies, near as they were to the rez, it wasn't unusual to get some rough trade even at this hour of the morning. After being held up five times in the past two years, he tended to be hypersensitive to suspicious looking characters like these. He fingered the butt of the revolver he kept on a shelf under the counter below the register. *They better not mess with me.*

To his right, a third man with a rusty red mullet strolled down the snack aisle. He wore an orange T-shirt, black jeans and scuffed along in unlaced army boots. He loaded up a plastic shopping basket with two boxes of doughnuts, every bag of beef jerky, and two cans of beef stew. "Tommy!" he yelled to the one at the front of the store.

Ed shifted his attention to the boy by the door. The kid leaned against the ATM machine, leafing through a *Hustler* magazine. He was decidedly younger than the other three. He had freckles, big ears and a shock of unruly red hair with a cowlick poking up from the middle of his head. The boy looked to be about nineteen and reminded the clerk of Alfred E. Neuman" from *Mad Magazine.*

"You want some of them vi-eenna sausages?" the Mullet called across the store. Tommy appeared too engrossed in the magazine to look up. "Tommy, you dumbass. Do you want these?" He held up the little can and wiggled it.

"Hell, yeah," the boy responded. "Grab me some mustard too, JP."

The clerk observed them closely and stored their descriptions in his head in case he'd need to file a police report later. Probably no need, but he'd learned his lesson in the past. The kid was Tommy. The Mullet was JP. *Tommy. JP.* Ed repeated the names in his head, burning them into his memory. On closer inspection, he determined that the four men were probably brothers. They all had similar red hair, tiny pig eyes, pock-marked faces and a shared ugliness that didn't speak well for their parents.

The earless one strolled to the counter. He was one ugly-looking jasper. His face looked like he'd lost an acid fight. Ed judged him to be a boxer who had taken more falls than he'd won. Maybe that explained the missing ear. His blob of a nose had been broken more than once, and he had beady eyes just like the others. Upon closer inspection, Ed was surprised to note that the color of the man's eyes was gray—like those of a wolf. He'd never seen gray eyes in a human before. They were cold and blank. Lifeless. A bleak chill ran down his spine.

The skin around the man's eyes was puffy, as were his cheeks which were rosy with broken blood vessels. The most shocking thing about him, though, was the gnarled stump on the side of his head where his ear had once been. A six-inch scar carved its way from his missing ear to just above his chin. As he approached, a sharp tang stung the clerk's nostrils. It wasn't just the man's pungent body odor. It smelled like evil.

He placed two beefy hands on the counter and gave Ed a broad grin. There was a gap in his smile where two side teeth were missing. Ed took a step back. He cleared his throat and quickly composed himself. "Good morning. Can I help you?" He noticed a slight squeak in his voice.

"You most certainly can," the man said with false amiability. His voice was deep and gravelly. It reminded the clerk of the low growl of a grizzly bear, protecting her cubs like the one that he had run across while hunting up in the Beartooths last fall. As frightening as that had been, he somehow felt more threatened by the fellow standing in front of him now. "Gimme a carton of Marlboros and four bottles of Jack Daniels."

The two other men drew up behind the earless one and set their groceries on the counter. The one called JP left the basket on the counter and strolled to the front door where he leaned against the magazine rack, folded his arms, and peered out onto the parking lot as if he was looking for something. Turning his attention back to Earless and Tattoo, Ed saw they both were looking intently at him. Once again, the hair on the back of his neck came to attention.

His hands trembled slightly as he put the cigarettes and the bottles of liquor next to the basket. He punched the prices of each item into the cash register, bagging them as he did. *Might be needing that gun after all,* he thought and tried to calculate how long it would take him to pull on these boys if he had to.

The younger one, Tommy, pulled a couple of the cheesier girlie magazines from the rack and brought them to the counter. "Get these too, Jesse." He grinned at the earless one.

Jesse. Jesse—earless. Ed's brain stored some more data. *Jesse, Tommy, JP and the Harelip.* He repeated the names several times in his head. Leering like that, Tommy was the spitting image of Alfred E. Neuman. The clerk tried unsuccessfully to stifle a nervous chuckle.

"What's so funny? You laughing at me?" The tattooed man with the harelip, squinted at him with one pig eye, speaking with that nasally way harelips talk.

"Nothing," said Ed, shifting his gaze away from the boy and back to the groceries. "I was just thinking with all that beef jerky and the Jack Daniels and stuff, you boys are going to have an interesting day. You going fishing, or camping or something? We got bait and licenses if you need 'em."

"That's none of your frickin business." The threatening tone of the harelip's statement lost some of its power and came out almost comically due to his garbled speech impediment. Once again, Ed found himself stifling a giggle.

The harelip glared at him, and one eye twitched. Ed bit his lip.

"Whoa, take it easy, Butch," said Jesse, putting a calming hand on Harelip's shoulder. "The man didn't mean no harm. Did you, old man?"

Butch. Butch—harelip. Tommy, JP, Jesse, Butch. "Course not. Sorry. I was just making an observation, that's all. Around here fishing and hunting is about all there is to do." Ed managed a bit of a smile. "Well, if that's it, I'll ring you up." He looked at the screen on his register and added, "And, looks like you boys filled up at pump number four, right? Let's see . . . " He tapped the total button, and the register drawer popped open with a ding. "The damage comes to one hundred and ninety-three dollars and eighty-seven cents."

From his position by the door, JP called, "Blue light just went by."

Tommy and Butch swiveled toward the front, but Jesse kept his gaze on the clerk. Even though he felt a weakness in his old knees, Ed remained focused on Jesse, and once again touched his index finger to the metal handle of his pistol.

Tommy turned with a wild-eyed look to his brother and said, "Shit, Jesse."

Still looking at Jesse, Ed said, "Will that be check or credit card? We still take cash too."

Jesse turned and patted his rear pocket. "I seem to have forgotten my wallet. Butch, you want to pay the man?"

Harelip smirked. "Sure, but I need my change first."

Ed could hear and feel each beat of his heart, pounding in his ear. His fingers inched across the pistol's handle. "Your change? Excuse me?"

With a quick movement, Butch drew a gun out of his waistband. "I'll take what you have in the register, old man."

The clerk's voice remained steady. He'd been here before. He inched his hand away from the pistol and slowly placed both hands palms down on the counter. "Now listen, son. You don't want to do this."

Jesse spoke up. "You're mistaken, old man. We do want to do this. And trust me, my brother is not a man you want to disappoint. Now, empty the till into a bag and hurry up."

Butch pulled back the hammer on his gun and sneered. "Yeah, don't disappoint me."

"Where's that blue light, JP?" Jesse called out.

"Long gone. Probably already at the donut shop pounding down his second chocolate covered." JP chuckled at his own joke so hard he snorted.

"Look, boys," said Ed with a slight quiver in his voice now. "I got less than a hundred bucks in the register. I don't want no trouble, and neither do you. So why don't you just leave the groceries, walk out, keep the gas, no charge, and I'll forget you were here."

Jesse reached across the counter and grabbed the clerk by the shirtfront. His breath was as evil as his body odor. "You don't understand. You see, we need these things and we have no money because we have just escaped from Deer Lodge where Butch here was doing life for murdering a family in Livingston and another fellow over in Three Forks. Now, believe me when I tell you, he has no problem killing you right now. I would prefer he didn't because it might attract the sheriff who just drove by. But," Jesse's voice took on an icy tone, and his gray eyes narrowed, "if you don't put the money in that bag right goddam now, I'll kill you myself."

A bead of sweat ran down the clerk's face, and his bladder let go, staining the front of his green work pants. His voice shook, and his breath came hard. "All right. Here—" With Jesse's hand still gripping the front of his shirt and his heart pounding, he took the few bills from the register and shoved them in the bag of groceries.

"Tommy. Butch." said Jesse, "Grab the groceries and let's go."

The boy scooped up the two bags. Butch tucked the pistol back in his belt and picked up the cases of beer, and they headed to the door.

Jesse released the clerk and said, "Do you have a cell phone?"

"No, sir."

"Good. We took the liberty of cutting your phone line before we came in. So, don't think about calling the sheriff. But I'm afraid I'm going to have to tie you up so we have enough time to put some space between us. I guess I should have had you charge us for this roll of duct tape too." He shook the roll of gray tape at the clerk and started to come around the counter.

As soon as Jesse moved in front of the fly-specked cabinet displaying greasy hot dogs, taquitos and fried gizzards, Ed drew his pistol and fired at Butch, the one with the gun. The explosion shook the windows of the convenience store, and Jesse dropped to his knees. The shot missed Butch and struck the boy, Tommy, in the back. The boy screamed and lurched forward, dropping the groceries. Vienna Sausage and beef stew cans clattered across the checkerboard linoleum.

Butch let out a hellish roar that turned Ed's blood to ice water. "You son of a bitch," cried Butch. He dropped the cases of beer, and in one move, pulled his gun, turned and fired at Ed. The impact of the bullet knocked the old man back against the display rack behind him. Packs of cigarettes cascaded down on top of his head. *What the hell?* He looked disbelievingly at the opening in his chest. Thick dark blood dribbled down his shirt front. *Dang, look at that hole. I'm shot. But it don't even hurt. Those sonsabitches. Those goddam sonsabitches.*

"Tommy!" called Jesse as he dashed to the boy's side.

Still wondering about his lack of pain, Ed looked up and saw JP take in what was happening, then run to the car and start the engine. He reached across and opened the passenger door, then pushed the seat back forward. "Come on," he yelled. "We gotta get the hell out of here."

Ed reached for the cleaning cloth and pressed it to his wound. The scene playing out before him swam dreamily as if he were watching it on a movie screen. Butch and Jesse caught Tommy by the armpits, dragged him outside and stuffed him into the back seat of the car. Butch got in the rear with him while Jesse jumped in front.

Gotta stop them. Ed's adrenaline pumped through his system like a jackhammer and pushed him from behind the counter. He began to be more aware of a deep pain rising from within him. His breath was harder to draw. With his gun in one hand and the other clasping the bloody cloth to his chest, he zigzagged to the front of the store. It felt as if he moved in hazy slow motion, almost like it wasn't even his body. His eyes stayed focused on the punks, but everything in his peripheral vision was a blur.

He lurched against a shelf, and candy bars and packs of donuts tumbled to the floor. His vision went dark, and he had to shake his head to get his sight back. He reached the door and stumbled outside as the red Mustang peeled out of the parking lot. *Mustang*, he stored in his brain. The pistol felt as if it weighed a hundred pounds as he tried to raise it and fire. Before he could get a shot off, a sharp hitch stabbed his chest, and he caught a last breath. Ed Loomis tumbled dead against the bundles of firewood for sale and collapsed to the ground. As he hit the sidewalk, the pistol fired and ricocheted off the pavement, striking the bottom of the retreating car.

The dirt and gravel thrown up by the car's rear tires settled over the old clerk's prone body like a dusty shroud.

Two

The sunlight inched its way up the eastern side of the mountains and broke over the ridge, sending warm rays onto the soft, pink eyelids of Heather Kimble who was smuggled up against her new husband, Steve. The heat from his body and the warm quilt covering her made her feel toasty and safe. But her nose was cold from the crisp and fragrant breeze wafting its way through the fir trees and into their bedroom window. She blinked awake and for a moment was confused about where she was.

It certainly wasn't back home in Ohio. She squinted out the window and caught her breath. The soaring snow-capped mountains and dark green Douglas firs outside were a far cry from the endless cornfields and flat farmlands she was used to. This place was glorious. Breathtaking. She inhaled deeply, savoring the fresh, clean air. A broad smile spread across her face.

When Mrs. Preston picked them up at the airport last night, she was so exhausted from everything. Twelve months of planning the wedding, one month of stressful final arrangements, cancellations, and last minute squabbles with her mother, her friends and Steve; the wedding itself—the beautiful wedding. Then there was the crazy reception where she ate too little and drank too much. Before she knew it, her girlfriends swept her away and got her dressed and packed for the honeymoon. They almost missed the flight out of Columbus and barely made their connection in Denver. As Steve waited at the baggage carousel at the airport in Kalispell, she fell asleep on the bench. She woke to Steve shaking her. Their bags sat next to an attractive older woman who introduced herself as Annie Preston, their host. She remembered Mrs. Preston was wearing a leather skirt, a plaid shirt and cowboy boots and had her hair in a long braid but beyond that, she couldn't call to mind any conversation with the woman. She dimly recalled getting in the green van with the Thief Creek Bed and Breakfast sign on it, but everything from that point on was a blur, except for the blissful comfort she felt as she sank into the blessed softness of the big log bed.

Heather sat up, stretched and took another deep breath of the marvelous mountain air. The view outside her window was spectacular. Craggy mountains reached high into the fluffy white clouds that dotted the amazing cornflower blue sky like giant cottony sheep. It was late June, but there was still plenty of snow along the ridge. Spiky green trees covered the bottom two-thirds of the mountains, and the final third was made up of giant boulders, gullies and shale fields. Magnificent. She sighed a happy sigh.

The bedroom walls were constructed of logs decorated with cowboy paraphernalia—spurs, a battered old high-crowned hat, a coiled lariat and rough-framed pictures of rodeo riders, cowgirls and buffalos. A large bouquet of what Heather assumed to be local wildflowers exploded in brilliant yellows, lavender, orange and reds from a pottery vase on the dresser.

It was all too wonderful. They were finally here in Montana, married and on their honeymoon. "Yeehaw!" Heather yelped.

Steve woke with a start. "What? What the . . ." The look of shock on his sleep-creased face made Heather burst out laughing.

Steve rubbed his eyes and ran his hand through his tousled black hair. "What the hell, Heather," he grumbled.

"Good morning, Dr. Kimble, my husband," Heather said, giving him a playful poke in the ribs.

"Ugh," Steve grunted and dropped back on to the pillow. He shaded his eyes from the brilliant sun now fully above the mountains. "Good morning, Mrs. Kimble. What time is it?"

Heather glanced at the digital clock next to the bed. "It's almost a quarter to seven, sleepyhead. Quarter to eight back home. Come on. Get up. We can go for a quick run before breakfast."

Steve got up on one arm and squinted at his wife. "A run? Really? Honey, I'm sorry. After yesterday, I'll be lucky if I get out of bed today."

"You have to get up. We're going horseback riding today. Remember? It's beautiful outside, and Montana is a beautiful place. And we'll feel beautiful after our run."

Steve grinned and said, "You're already beautiful, sweetheart. I'm the luckiest man alive. But I'm also the tiredest man alive. Go for a run, babe. I'm going to catch a little more shut-eye before breakfast. I'll run with you this evening. I promise."

Heather pouted dramatically then leaned over him and shook her curly blonde hair in his face. "Okay, lazybones." She threw back the quilt and hopped out of bed. The cold air felt like someone poured a bucket of ice water over her naked body. She clutched herself and pranced to her suitcase. "Brrrr," she shivered. "I'm all goosebumpy. Look."

She turned to see that Steve was already admiring her body and grinning lewdly.

"I think you should come back to bed. Now," he said. "I'll warm you up."

"Too late," she said. "You missed your chance. Maybe you'll get lucky after breakfast before they pick us up to go riding."

Steve groaned and pulled her pillow over his head.

Heather turned and examined herself in the mirror. She was proud of her body. She had to admit she was very hot. As a physical trainer and karate instructor, she needed to stay in excellent shape. She admired her firm breasts, her flat stomach, and then turned to check out her tight, round buns. Not an ounce of body fat. Her arms and legs were well-toned. It took a lot of effort to stay in such great shape, but she loved exercise, working out in the gym, hiking, running, rock climbing, biking. Indoors or outdoors, she could spend hours happily sculpting the beautiful machine that was her body as well as helping others achieve their physical goals.

Heather slipped into a pair of running shorts and pulled a light pink sweatshirt over her head. She laced up her New Balances, wrapped a rubber band around her hair and ran her ponytail through the back of a pink baseball cap.

"My God, you're hot. Please come back in here," Steve whined from the bed. He threw back the quilt, and she saw that he was more than eager to have her join him.

"Well, good morning, Doctor!" Heather's big blue eyes widened at the sight. Ignoring his offer, she hiked her leg up onto the top of the dresser and stretched her calves, well aware that she was torturing the poor guy. "Sorry, Hon, but I'm all dressed and ready to go. I'll see you when I get back."

Pouting, Steve threw the comforter back over himself. "Well, you'd better hurry."

She laughed, bent and kissed him. "I love you," she called as she let herself out of the room.

"Love you," Steve grumbled back.

The hallway walls of the old inn were covered with framed pictures— aged sepias and black and whites of rodeo riders on bucking broncos and cowboys branding calves. Heather admired the Charles M. Russell prints and original oil paintings of Indians and fur-capped mountain men. *What a wild and wonderful place*, she thought to herself.

She bounced down the stairs two at a time, eager to start her run. She leapt from the last two steps to the entryway just as a man came around the corner holding a steaming carafe of coffee and nearly collided with him.

"Oops," he chuckled and pulled the coffeepot out of the way.

Heather's cheeks reddened. "Excuse me. I'm so sorry."

The man smiled broadly. He had a kind and rugged face, longish gray hair with a short ponytail tied in the back. A small splash of coffee stained the front of his plaid shirt, and a few drops dappled his blue jeans. "Not a problem," he laughed. "Occupational hazard. Soon I'll be splattered with bacon grease and eggs. You must be Heather. I'm Mike. Nice to meet you. Looks like you're headed for a run."

Heather shook his hand. "Oh, you're Mr. Preston. It's nice to meet you. "

"Please call me Mike. Sorry I wasn't up to greet you and Steve last night. I was working on my darn truck until late. Never did get it running. Annie woke me when she got back from picking you guys up at the airport, but I'm afraid I was too lazy to get up. Where's your new husband? Are you running away from him already?"

Heather chuckled and pointed her thumb up the stairs. "Steve's still up in bed. It was a long day yesterday. I thought I'd get a quick run in before breakfast. Do I have time?"

"Oh, sure. You two are our only guests this week. How long a run are you going for? You know, we're at eight thousand feet here. If you're not used to it, the altitude can do a number on you."

"I'll just take a short run. Is half an hour okay?"

Mike smiled and nodded. "Breakfast will be ready when you're done with your shower. Don't forget that the wrangler from the Double J Ranch is picking you two up at ten."

"I know. I'm so excited. I've always wanted to go horseback riding. And it's so gorgeous here in the mountains." Heather checked her watch. "I better get going. I like trail running. Are there any trails around here you'd recommend?"

"There are lots of trails around here, but, I'd suggest you stick to the road. Wait a minute." Mike held up his hand, then disappeared into the kitchen. He re-emerged with a thin black canister and handed it to her. She crinkled her nose questioningly.

"Here. Take this with you. It's bear spray. I saw a black bear with her cubs in the timber up behind the inn yesterday. She's been hanging around foraging for a couple of weeks. You probably won't run into her, but stay on the road. And keep alert. It's springtime, and the bears are hungry and feisty. "

Heather took the spray can with wide eyes and gulped. "Maybe I shouldn't go."

The innkeeper smiled and said, "Don't worry. Enjoy your run. You'll be okay. The bears are more scared of you than you are of them. It's not likely you'll see them. It doesn't hurt to be cautious, though. If you need to, just point the can at the bear and press this trigger. Aim for the eyes. And whatever you do, don't try to outrun them. They can run up to thirty-five miles per hour. If you come across one and the spray doesn't chase it away, some people say you should lie down and play dead. Others say you should call out to it and make a loud noise. Stand as tall as you can and make yourself look as big as possible. Black bears prefer to avoid humans and will generally try to avoid getting involved with them unless it's a sow protecting her cubs."

Heather inspected the can in her hand and hesitated before reaching for the doorknob. The excited adrenaline she felt earlier at the prospect of her run had turned to a touch of nervous anxiety. She looked back at Mike with a furrowed brow and one questioning eyebrow raised.

"Go on now," he said and opened the door for her. "I'll have a great breakfast waiting for you when you get back."

She gave him a wan smile, then turned and gripping the bear spray tightly in her hand, jogged up to the road, craning her head in all directions as she went.

THREE

Annie Preston heard the ambulance take the corner off Main and watched it drive up Second Street to the clinic. The siren was on, but the vehicle moved at regular speed. She had heard the sheriff's car and the ambulance tearing down Main Street earlier and was curious what had happened. It looked as if she was about to find out.

"Emma," she called over her shoulder. "You need to get out here."

"I'm in the bathroom." Emma sounded annoyed, as usual.

"I know, but they're bringing someone in, and I could use your help."

A heavy sigh. "All right, I'll be out in a minute."

Annie heard the toilet flush as the ambulance came to a stop out front. The two EMTs exited, swung open the back doors and pulled the stretcher out. The legs of the stretcher unfolded, and the men wheeled it toward the clinic doors. Their movements were unhurried, and Annie felt a nervous lump drop in her stomach. *Now what*, she thought.

Emma emerged from the bathroom reeking of cigarette smoke. As she came out, she flipped the light switch off but left the exhaust fan whirring. Annie bit her lip to keep from telling her for the thousandth time that if she was going to smoke she'd have to do it outside, not in the bathroom.

Emma peered out front while she dug in her uniform and adjusted her bra strap. "Who is it?"

Annie shook her head. "I don't know. Come on. Get the door."

The two women pulled open the front doors, and the EMTs rolled the stretcher by them. The sheet was pulled up over the patient's face, and a large blood stain spread across the top of the sheet.

"Back there?" the EMT gestured with his head to the examining room.

"Yes," said Annie. "Who is it?"

"Ed Loomis. Gunshot to the chest. He's dead."

"Oh my God. Ed Loomis?" gasped Emma clasping a hand to her ample bosom.

Annie pictured the old clerk chattering behind the counter at the Gas-N-Go. He was a bit of a curmudgeon, but a harmless coot, just another Lame Elk character. Why would anyone shoot him? "What happened?"

They rolled the stretcher into the middle of the examining room and unbuckled the holding straps. "Robbery," said the older EMT. "Sheriff said they cleaned out the register and shot old Ed. He was lying outside the store with a gun in his hand. Musta chased after them. Carl Jurgens was across the street in the hardware store and said he heard the gunshots and saw a red Mustang taking off down Main Street."

Emma waddled to the head of the stretcher and pulled back the sheet. "Poor Ed," she said and shook her head.

The EMTs took up positions at the top and bottom of the stretcher and were about to lift the body onto the examining table when there was a commotion out in the lobby.

"Just a minute," said Annie holding up her hand. She went out to the front desk where she saw a rancher in dusty jeans holding a dirty rag around his hand. He paced up and down cursing under his breath. Another younger cowboy watched him anxiously and rushed over to her as she came round the corner.

"Can I help you ?" she said.

The young man bobbed his head. "My dad cut his hand real bad. His thumb's just hanging there."

The older man strode over to her holding out his wounded hand. Annie gently unwrapped the oily rag and saw the deep cut across the base of his thumb. A flock of butterflies rose in her stomach and fluttered around her heart, but she maintained a calm voice and carefully re-wrapped the bloody hand.

"Just a moment, please. I'll be right with you." She hurried back to the examining room where the two EMTs stood waiting by the stretcher.

"Emma," she said, "have these men take Mr. Loomis to the back room for now. I'm going to need this room for the man who just came in."

Emma led the EMTs down the hall with Ed's body. Annie wiped her hand across her forehead and blew a loose strand of hair from her face. *It's going to be one of those days.* She took a deep breath, tucked her hair behind her ear and headed out to the front desk.

"Okay, she smiled, "would you like to come with me?" The grimacing rancher and his son crossed the lobby and followed Annie to the examining room.

FOUR

The Toomey brothers' Mustang barreled down the state highway at top speed. JP drove and had the accelerator jammed to the floor. He hadn't slowed down since they'd left Lame Elk. From the passenger seat, Jesse James Toomey watched his brother with concern. JP was hunched over the steering wheel. The veins on his hands and his knuckles bulged as he gripped the wheel like he wanted to strangle it. His eyes darted from the road to the rearview mirror and back. Jesse thought of saying something to JP to slow him down, but he himself was feeling anxious about their situation. He turned his focus on the road ahead and tried to block out the anguished moans of his brother, Tommy, writhing in pain in the back seat.

"Try to quit squirming around, Tommy," Butch said. He had removed his shirt and pressed it on the hole in his younger brother's back to stanch the blood.

Tommy blubbered and twisted in Butch's arms. "Oh, God, it hurts so bad, Butchy. Oh, God. Am I going to die?"

"If you keep jerking around you fucking will. Lie still for crissake."

Jesse leaned over the seat and put a calming hand on Tommy's leg. "You ain't going to die. We'll get you taken care of. Try to take it easy."

Tommy's tear-filled eyes bugged out with fear and pain. "Don't let me die, Jesse."

Jesse managed a weak smile and said, "I won't let you die, Tommy. Don't worry. Have I ever let you down? You just hang in there. Everything's going to be all right." He glanced at Butch whose own face had gone white and showed little belief that everything was going to be all right.

Jesse turned back and spoke to JP in a low voice. "We've got to get him somewhere fast."

"What the hell do you want me to do?" JP snapped. "The closest town is back there, and all that's there is the Gas-N-Go with a dead clerk in the parking lot. The cops are probably already on our ass. Want me to turn around and ask them where the nearest hospital is?" He cast a worried glance at the rearview mirror. "There's nothing around here for at least a hundred miles. I don't even know how to get on the interstate from here. What the—? Crap."

"What now?" asked Jesse rolling his eyes. JP's attitude was really starting to piss him off.

"We're almost out of gas."

"Bullshit. We just tanked up back there."

"Well, I don't know what to tell you. This says we're on empty."

Jesse followed his brother's gaze and saw that the needle on the gas gauge had slipped over the E. An orange light warned they were nearly out of fuel. "Shit, what next? How the hell . . .?" He mulled over the possible answers to this new dilemma. "The old man took a shot at us as we were driving away. He must have hit the gas tank. That's just great." Jesse pounded his fist on the dashboard.

"Shit, Tommy," said Butch from the backseat, his nasally voice trembling. "He's passed out. Or dead."

Jesse looked at his younger brother leaning against the back window. He swiveled and placed his fingers on the boy's neck for a moment. "He's not dead. He's just passed out. At least that will keep him from moving for a while. Keep that shirt tight against his body."

He leaned his head against the seat back and looked out the window at the high walls of the canyon whizzing past and tried to think what to do. Just like his namesake, the outlaw Jesse James, after whom his father had named him, he was the idea man. The leader. Although Butch was the eldest, in Jesse's opinion, he himself was the only one with any brains. Tommy, JP and Butch looked to him to have all the answers. It was always up to him. JP and Butch were too stupid to think for themselves. If it wasn't for him, they'd still be back in Deer Lodge Prison. He's the one who had come up with the plan to escape. He was the one who had talked Tommy into making the arrangement with his friend and to have him waiting for them in his Mustang with the gun. Last night when JP wanted to keep driving to Idaho, it was he who had to think straight and convince those morons that that would get them caught. That every road would be crawling with cops. It was his idea to hole up in that abandoned barn till morning. Then again, if it hadn't been for him, Tommy wouldn't be bleeding out in the back seat. Now it would be up to him to fix this mess.

Poor Tommy. Unlike his brothers, Tommy had managed to stay out of trouble all these years. JP and Jesse had been in and out of the joint since eighth grade for theft, armed robbery and various other crimes. Butch was the real bad ass. Convicted of four murders. Guilty, but never convicted, of rape and several other unsolved crimes, Butch was the most dangerous of the Toomey boys. A good muscle man, but dumb as a brick. A psychopath, according to the prosecuting attorney's medical expert. JP? He was just JP. Did what he was told. Whined too much, but he was obedient. Tommy, though, had always been the one hope of the family. He'd even finished a year of community college. Now the kid was lying in the back seat bleeding to death. If Pop were alive today, he'd pistol whip Jesse for sure, or worse, for dragging the kid into this.

He had to think. Think. He rubbed his forehead trying to quiet the dull throb. There was only one road and one direction they could go in and no gas stations. If they couldn't get Tommy patched up soon, they would lose him for sure. If they could have just made it to Idaho like he planned, they could have hooked up with his old cellmate, Johnnie Servideo, who was magic with bullet wounds. But now they were running out of gas and running out of time.

"So what the hell are we going to do?" asked JP looking over at Jesse.

Suddenly, the Mustang took a sharp curve and skidded, spewing gravel and rocks to the side of the road. Jesse's stomach clenched. JP jerked the wheel back under control as the car's rear end twisted back and forth.

"Jesus, JP," Jesse said. "Just shut up and keep your eyes on the damn road. You're gonna kill us." At the speed they were traveling, they might all end up dead. They streaked past three white crosses grouped together at the edge of the steep embankment. That was the Montana Highway Department's way of highlighting spots as fatal accident sites. Jesse's heartbeat pounded in his ears.

Just up the road was a small brown sign. Jesse leaned forward and strained to read it as it came into view and then disappeared. It was a rustic wood sign with a log cabin painted on it that read Thief Creek Bed and Breakfast—10 Miles. "Hey, there's a place ten miles up ahead. Turn in there."

JP, who was focused on keeping on the road said, "Where? What are you talking about? There's nothing out here."

"Didn't you see that sign?"

JP shook his head.

"It said there's a bed and breakfast up ahead. We'll take Tommy there. Fix him up. Maybe we can boost a car."

JP raised an eyebrow. "A bed and breakfast? Oh, that will be so nice. We can have tea and freaking crumpets while the guests sew up Tommy and call the sheriff. How sweet."

Jesse leaned into his brother's face and hissed, "You got a better idea? Tommy's bleeding to death, for crissake. We've got to take care of him, and we've got to ditch this car."

"Just do it, JP. We've got no choice," Butch said.

"I don't like it. How do you know—"

Butch leaned over Tommy and smacked the back of JP's head so hard he knocked him against the side window. The car swerved again.

"Son of a bitch," JP said and rubbed the back of his head.

"You heard him. Just do it," said Butch.

In the distance, they saw a small sign at the entrance to a gravel road. When they got close enough to read it, it said simply, THIEF CREEK ROAD.

"This has got to be it," said Jesse. "Take a right."

JP almost missed the turn and slammed on the brakes, fishtailing around the corner. The Toomey brothers all lurched to the left. Tommy let out a muffled groan from the back seat.

Just ahead another sign similar to the first one with the log cabin said, "Thief Creek B&B—15 mi." with an arrow pointing up the road.

JP said, "It's 15 more miles. I don't think we're gonna make it."

"Shutup and just keep driving," said Jesse. He looked ahead and to the sides and nodded. "This is good. Nice and remote."

With a cloud of dust forming a curling contrail behind it, the Mustang galloped its desperate way up the winding mountain road to the Thief Creek Bed and Breakfast.

FIVE

Heather was back in fifteen minutes. Mike was in the dining room setting the table and waved at her. "That was quick," he said. "How far did you go?"

"Not very." She set the bear spray down on the dining room table. "Thanks for this. The views are really incredible up here in the mountains. But," a rosy blush colored her cheeks, "I got nervous about seeing bears and decided I'd take a run later with Steve."

Mike chuckled. "I'm sorry if I scared you about the bears. We pretty much take them for granted around here. As I said, it's not likely you'll run into any. It's just a good idea to carry bear spray with you when you're in the back country. Can I get you a cup of coffee?"

Heather looked back toward the stairs. "I guess I should let Steve get a few more minutes of sleep. I'd love a cup. It smells delicious. Coffee is pretty much my only vice."

"Vice?" exclaimed Mike, pouring her a mug. "Back where we're from its considered illegal not to drink it. Sugar or cream?"

"No thanks." She took a sip of the strong black brew and said, "Where are you from?"

"Annie and I are from the Seattle area. She's a nurse, and I used to teach college English."

"Seattle? What brought you out here?"

Mike folded the napkins into crisp triangles and placed them next to the dishes. "We moved here four years ago. We'd vacationed in Montana several times over the years and fell in love with it. We saw the Thief Creek Inn advertised for sale and decided that living up here in the mountains was where we wanted to be. I'd had enough of academia, and Annie was tired of the city. So here we are."

"I don't blame you. The inn sure is lovely. So quiet."

Mike nodded. "We like it. It was built in the early 1930s as a hunting lodge by a wealthy businessman from Minneapolis. He's the reason for the trophies hanging in the Great Room." He pointed to the snarling bobcat, the bearded white mountain goat, the massive buffalo head, and various deer and elk mounts displayed high up on the walls. "Annie's not crazy about them, but they are as much a part of the history of this place and its surroundings as the logs they hang from."

Mike filled her in on the background of the inn and pointed out some of its highlights. He was proud of the old lodge and its rich mountain ambience. He and Annie had been caring stewards of the place. The floor to ceiling leaded glass windows sparkled in the dining room and the Great Room. They were adorned with intricate metal work in the forms of the local flora and fauna of the Rocky Mountains. Each pane of glass was framed by hand-wrought lodgepole pines, cottonwoods, aspen trees, wolves, bears, mountain lions, moose, elk, deer or leaping trout. The hand-hewn log walls were twenty inches thick and gleamed from the recent oiling he had given them. In the Great Room, between the two tallest windows, a huge fireplace with massive cast iron andirons sat at the base of a wall made of large rounded river rock that climbed the two stories of the room. On top of the heavy log mantel sat a collection of framed photos of proud hunters kneeling next to their catches. There were also pictures of smiling families and friends of long ago posing in front of the lodge in baggy old ski outfits or holding fly fishing rigs in one hand and stringers of trout in the other. In the center of the wall above the mantel, a shotgun hung on two shiny brass hooks. The wide plank floors were also carefully maintained and waxed faithfully every four weeks. Two brown leather couches formed a conversation ell in front of the fireplace.

Mike's favorite spot was the substantial overstuffed chair and hassock that snuggled into the corner of the Great Room and offered those seated in it a panorama of the interior—the dining room, Great

Room, and the Sunroom beyond. From the comfort of the seat one was also treated to a magnificent picture window with an outside view of the short hillside below that dropped down to the timber where a well-worn game trail wound along Thief Creek. It was a rare day that you didn't see a group of deer, elk or the occasional moose strolling down to the silvery water that bubbled over its cobbled bed of stone. Beyond the trees, there was the spectacular grandeur of the soaring mountains. Their majesty always offered something breathtaking to look at, whether it was the icing of snow along their ridge for much of the year, the breathtaking Alpenglow of orange, violet and red in the morning, or the mirage they offered that one could almost touch the giant white clouds that seemed to float just inches above the summits. Guests coveted the seat for reading, knitting or simply resting and renewing their souls as they gazed out upon the awesome natural beauty of Montana.

Heather sipped her coffee as Mike extolled the features within and outside the inn. "It is just wonderful here. I'm so glad we came." She sniffed and turned her gaze toward the kitchen. "Where is Mrs. Preston? Is she cooking? It smells delicious."

"Thanks. That's my cooking. Annie is in Lame Elk. She works in the clinic there two days a week."

"Wow, isn't that quite a commute?"

Mike nodded. "You bet. She leaves early in the morning and doesn't get back till pretty late at night. It's only two times a week, though, and the extra money is nice. Lame Elk is so small there aren't any other nurses around, and the doctor is only part time himself. So, Annie is often the only healthcare professional available, and is always in high demand."

Heather nodded her head. "I can imagine. Steve has just started working as a doctor at a hospital with all kinds of physicians, specialists and nurses, and he's swamped all the time. We were lucky to get this week off for our honeymoon."

"Well," said Mike, "Lame Elk is a lot smaller than where you're from, I'm sure, but they keep Annie busy. They are lucky to have her.

The only bad thing is that she's got the van, so I'm stuck. My truck is on the fritz, and I have to pick up some parts. The closest place to get them is Whitefish, and that's about an hour and a half from here. I'll have to wait till Saturday when I can take the van."

A buzzer interrupted their conversation. Mike excused himself and disappeared into the kitchen. The oven door squeaked open, and a fragrant, heady cloud filled the room with the warm aroma of the sausage casserole.

Mike called out, "Breakfast should be ready in about fifteen minutes. You ought to go roust up your hubby."

"Yum. I'm starving. I'll go get Steve, and we'll be right down." Heather put the coffee cup on the table, turned and bounded up the stairs.

❧   ❧   ❧

Mike checked the kitchen clock and put the egg and sausage casserole in the warming drawer of the oven. He shook his head and grinned. *Newlyweds*, he thought. Heather had gone upstairs saying she'd be right down. That was half an hour ago. No matter, they had plenty of time for breakfast if they wanted it. The van from the Double J wouldn't be picking them up till ten. He was used to honeymooners skipping breakfast. He just hated to waste the food.

He picked up her mug from the table and rinsed it in the sink. As he did so, he gazed out at the tall lodgepole pines and the high mountains rising up behind the inn. The endless blue sky was clear and clean save for a small rain cloud far to the south. That was okay. They could always use the rain. As a largely agricultural state and one subject to forest fires, Montana precipitation, whether rain or snow, was all too rare and always welcome. Mike mused about their days in Seattle when all it seemed to do was rain. It was a whole different world back then.

He thought back to those days of constant stress and struggle. The heavy gray dampness of Seattle weighed on him like the plodding and maddening bureaucracy and political gamesmanship of being a university professor. Years of fruitless work and ass-kissing of pompous deans and incompetent chairpeople for that coveted tenure position that never came. His frustration and inability to control his own situation gnawed at him like a cancer and infected even his marriage.

The early years for them had been as idealistic, romantic and hopeful as what he now saw in Heather's bright face. Like newlyweds everywhere, he and Annie had faced the world with optimism and joy, confident in themselves and the steadfastness of their love for each other. But eventually, the tedious years of life on the campus took their toll. For Annie, the crazy hours she worked at the hospital left her little energy or patience for him. At first, she was supportive during his awakening to the mind-numbing realities of the foot-dragging ineptitude and political horse crap he had to deal with on a daily basis. She encouraged him to keep going and fight the good fight. But as time plodded on and inexorably wore him down, she became less interested in hearing him whine and rail against the rulers in the ivory tower of the university who kept him dancing on a string, semester after semester, year after year.

It wasn't Annie's fault. She had her own trials to deal with at the hospital. The long hours, the administration, the lack of respect of the doctors toward the nurses, and the heartbreak of losing patients. Yet, she managed with aplomb. She carried on no matter what, doing what had to be done without complaint. She had an inner strength and confidence that he admired and respected, and if he was honest, was even a little jealous of. When confronted with a problem, Annie would tackle it head on then move on. She had some of her old man's stubborn hard-headedness. While he, sadly, had inherited his own father's penchant to suffer silently in sullen inactivity.

Over the years, their different approaches to their situations gradually caused an invisible wall to creep up between them. The passionate flame of their early love burned down to quietly smoldering embers that continued to glow dully beneath the ashes. There remained a shared warmth between them, but little effort was made by either one to stoke it into the fire it once was.

Thankfully, before even the embers burned out, Annie took the bull by the horns and insisted that they re-evaluate their lives and their marriage. It was she who had recommended the therapeutic vacation in Montana where they would be surrounded by big sky and sunshine away from the drab sameness of their Seattle life. Over ten glorious days in the natural freshness of the Rocky Mountains they found their souls renewed and their dwindling feelings reawakened for each other, for their marriage. They talked. They listened. They played. They laughed. They loved, again.

By the end of their vacation, they knew they could not go back to the soul-draining lives they had led. When a breakfast conversation with the owners of the bed and breakfast they were staying at revealed that the inn was for sale, a hasty conference over dinner was enough to convince them that this could be one of those life-changing opportunities meant for them to jump at. Within eight weeks they sold their house, packed up twenty years of "stuff," gave away or sold the rest, bid farewell to their friends and the city, and with happy hearts headed to their new, peaceful life in the mountains.

Now, instead of fighting with self-important deans and grading poorly written student papers, he was rinsing coffee cups and making fancy breakfasts. His biggest concerns were getting the chemicals right for the hot tub and making sure they had a good supply of toilet paper and eggs. Instead of the bustle and noise of rush hour traffic, all he heard these days was the busy chattering of the squirrels and the morning gossiping of the finches starting their day. He missed their friends and the wealth of great restaurants in Seattle, but the peace and solitude they had swapped for was more than worth it. They had a little piece of paradise now, and life was good. There wasn't a day he took for granted.

Mike was drawn out of his reverie as he heard his guests coming down the stairs. Heather arrived first with a post-coital flush to her cheeks. She had changed into jeans and her Ohio State University T-shirt. Steve's cheeks were also ruddy, and he had a rumpled look about him. Barefoot and with a cowlick in his dark hair, he strolled into the dining room tucking his wrinkled shirt into his blue jeans.

"Sorry we're late," said Heather with a self-conscious smile as she nestled into her chair.

Steve held out his hand to Mike and said, "Good morning."

Mike shook and said, "Good morning, Steve. I'm Mike. I hope you slept all right."

"Like a rock," replied Steve. "That log bed is comfortable. Are all the rooms that nice?"

"I think so. If you like, after breakfast I can show you two around."

"That would be great. This place is awesome. That buffalo head on the wall is cool. I noticed the stuff in the cabinet in the hallway. Are you a hunter?"

"Me? No. Most of those things—the traps, bows and arrows and stuff were in that display case when we bought the inn. Some of them are over a hundred years old. My father-in-law bought me the shotgun over the fireplace hoping I'd become a hunter like him." He chuckled to himself as he thought about what Annie's macho dad would think if he knew her husband was a dues-paying member of the Sierra Club and a big supporter of gun control legislation. "I've got a box of shells somewhere too, but I think I only used a couple of them to test out the gun. The kick just about knocked my arm off my shoulder."

He pointed at the sideboard with his chin. "There's coffee and cups over there. Help yourselves. I'll get your breakfasts right up."

Mike entered the kitchen and fixed their plates. Egg and sausage casserole, wheat toast and a careful arrangement of mixed berries with a sprig of bright green, fresh mint from the garden. He finished the presentation by sprinkling a light dusting of finely-chopped parsley around the bright white edges of the plates and brought them to the table.

"Wow," said Heather and Steve simultaneously as he set the meal before them. The warm smell of breakfast filled the dining room with a comforting aroma.

"Enjoy," said Mike. "There's homemade huckleberry jam in that dish over there."

Heather spread a large dollop of jam on her toast and took a bite. "Mmmm. Did you say this is homemade?"

"Yes. Annie made it from some berries we picked last fall."

"Do you do all the cooking?"

Mike nodded. "The cooking, the cleaning, the marketing and just about everything else. Annie is busy with her job and doesn't get home till late. So, I do pretty much everything here. I love it though. It's peaceful, and I don't have any of the aggravations my friends have back in the city. My biggest hassles are keeping the bears away from my trash. No fights with bosses, no rush hour traffic. My closest neighbor is over five miles away. The guests are always pleasant, and they enjoy the surroundings as much as I do."

"Do you ever get any jerks staying with you?" Steve asked with a mouthful of toast.

"Not so far. This isn't the kind of place that jerks have on their itinerary."

Mike poured himself a cup of coffee and topped off their cups. He pulled out a chair and sat down to join them. The three chatted amiably through the meal about the wedding, the couple's plans for their vacation, places that they wanted to explore and questions they had.

"So, what do you do back in Ohio? Heather mentioned you're a doctor?" Mike asked the pair.

Steve had a mouthful of casserole. He nodded and pointed his fork at Heather to explain.

She placed her hand on her husband's and said, "Steve has been doing his internship at the hospital in Columbus. He's a new doctor." She smiled at him with obvious pride in her eyes. "I teach karate and women's self-defense at a health club downtown. We both keep pretty busy and don't get much time to spend together, so we've been looking forward to this honeymoon for a long time. We just want to relax and have fun. No cell phones, no internet, no beepers."

"Well," said Mike, "this is the perfect place for that."

Steve swallowed the last of the casserole, placed his fork on the empty plate and wiped his mouth on the napkin. "That was great. Thanks. It was delicious." He patted his stomach and let out a gratified sigh. "You and your wife are really lucky. It seems like you've found yourselves a little piece of heaven."

Mike collected their plates and the rest of the breakfast things and headed to the kitchen. "I agree. I can't imagine a quieter, more peaceful way of life."

Six

The Mustang jolted along the washboard surface, thumping every few feet in and out of washed-out ruts and swerving as the tires did their best to hold the ragged road. Springtime driving in the mountains before the roads are graded is treacherous. Winter run-off carves deep gullies exposing axle-breaking rocks and creating putty-like mud the locals refer to as gumbo that cakes up on the tires, disabling any traction.

"Slow the hell down," Jesse yelled, steadying one hand against the dashboard. His jaw clenched as the front tire slid within inches of the steep drop-off on his side of the narrow road.

"I'm trying to get to the place before we run out of gas," JP snapped back, eyeing the plunging needle on the gas gauge.

The front end nosedived into a deep pothole, jolting the passengers off their seats. The car rocked back and forth. Tommy let out a tortured scream from the back seat. Jesse turned to check on him and saw Butch snatch his seatbelt and quickly buckle it up. "Keep that pressure on Tommy's wound, or he'll bleed out."

"I'm trying," Butch fired back and tried to regain his hold on the bloody shirt. "But JP's driving like a frigging maniac." As if to reinforce Butch's trepidation, The tire slammed into a melon-sized rock, jarring him into the side of the car.

Jesse's tailbone jammed against the car seat. "Ow. JP, for crissake, slow down."

Bent over the steering wheel and peering at the road ahead, JP struggled to keep control of the car. "Shut up. It's this freaking road. I'm doing the best I—"

Suddenly, the car fishtailed. The back tires skidded toward the side of the road. JP turned into the slide, but that only caused the front tires to slip into a gummy patch of mud and lose their purchase.

Jesse watched in horror as they side-slipped across the road. He put his hands in front of him on the dash. Both feet pushed against a non-existent brake pedal on the floor as the Mustang slid out of control toward the edge and the yawning drop below. The front tires dropped over the brink, and his stomach dropped at the same time.

"Oh, my God" rolled out of Jesse's mouth as if all his senses were operating in slow motion; he felt and heard the bottom of the car thump and scrape the last edge of the road. For a moment, the vast sky was all that appeared in the windshield, then a sickening gorge roared up from his stomach as he felt and saw the car pitch sideways down the steep embankment. JP crashed against him, and a sharp pain tore through his shoulder as he smashed against the door frame with the first rollover.

The Toomeys tumbled against each other cursing and screaming, colliding into the roof and the windows as the car somersaulted and pounded over boulders and brush. The world exploded in a chaotic kaleidoscope of sky, rocks, dirt, pain and noises, overwhelming Jesse's consciousness. He felt the pummeling would never stop when, with a vicious crash, the windshield burst into a spray of diamonds and the battered hunk of metal slammed to a halt against a cottonwood tree.

The noise and confusion melted into a hazy fog. It took a moment for Jesse to get his bearings. "Son of a bitch." He wasn't sure if it was himself or someone else who had sworn. His shoulder ached, and his head throbbed. His arm was crushed against the door. He clenched and unclenched his fingers and shifted his arm. Not broken, he registered with relief. The dashboard was bent and pressing against his knee, but he felt no pain in his leg. He raised his hand to the side of his head and felt a tender golf ball-sized lump developing, but no blood. *Holy crap*, he sighed.

He became aware of the sound of the motor running. JP's foot was still on the gas, and the engine revved, but the tires couldn't catch. The car was pinned against the tree with the driver's side wheels spinning uselessly off the ground and the passenger side spewing clods of dirt and rock into the air behind them.

He tried to bull his door open, but it was jammed tight against the tree. A spark of pain ran up his bruised arm.

Tommy moaned in the back seat. Jesse turned his head and saw blood draining out of the boy like syrup from a bottle. A whirlwind of conflicting emotions and questions stormed through him. Was anything broken? Were his brothers all right? Was Tommy dead? Why the hell didn't that asshole JP listen to him about slowing down? What the hell are we going to do now? His shoulder and head pounded with both physical and psychic pain.

JP had been thrown against him, and leaned heavily on his left side."Get the hell off me," he said and shoved at JP. However, his brother had apparently knocked himself unconscious when he hit the windshield and wasn't moving.

"Butch, you okay?" he yelled to be heard above the whining engine.

"Yeah, I'm all right. Tommy's passed out again. He's not doing good at all. He ain't gonna make it. What about JP?"

"Unconscious." Jesse kicked JP's leg knocking his foot off the accelerator, and the car quieted down."Get him off me so I can get out."

The engine sputtered, coughed twice, then died.

"Great," said Jesse. "That must have been the last of the gas. This is one big cluster."

Butch worked his way around and over Tommy, laying him gently against the side of the car, then maneuvered himself out of the back seat and onto the ground.

"I'm going to right the car first," he warned Jesse. As he said it, Butch closed the door, reached inside the window, gripped the steering wheel, and with a mighty tug, pulled the car back on all four wheels. JP fell back against his door, and Jesse slammed into him. Butch opened the door, and JP dropped against him and opened his eyes. Jesse saw a large red lump erupting on his forehead.

"Nice driving," Butch said as he pulled the dazed JP out and sat him on the ground.

Jesse struggled out of the front seat and checked himself for damage. Amazingly, other than a small bump on the side of his head and a badly bruised shoulder he seemed to have survived the rollover intact.

Butch flipped the back seat up and hauled Tommy out. He rested the wounded boy against the outside of the car next to JP and plugged the bullet hole as well as he could with what was left of his shirt. He looked up at the wrecked car, then at Jesse."What are we going to do now?"

Jesse glanced up the slope above them. "The B and B can't be much farther. You stay here with JP and Tommy. Keep him shaded. I'll hike up there and get a car and come back for you."

He crawled across the front seat and took the pistol and what was left of the shells out of the glove compartment. Jesse reloaded the gun and tucked it in his belt. He threw a last glance at the pitiful scene of his three brothers leaning against the trashed Mustang then headed for the climb.

Jesse struggled up the wall of scree on all fours, cursing every time the sharp rocks cut into his hands. About a third of the way to the top, he heard a vehicle crunching its way up the mountain road. He looked up at the edge of the road and back down at the mangled car. It didn't appear that the accident could be seen from the road above. *That's good,* he thought. *Best that no one spots them and reports it to the sheriff.*

He checked to make sure the gun was covered by his shirt, then doubled his effort to scramble up the steep pitch, ignoring the blades of flint that tore at his clothes and body. *Got to get that car,* became the mantra that pushed him on.

He almost reached the top, when he heard the vehicle drive by. A cloud of dust and tiny pebbles rained down on him as the vehicle grumbled overhead and continued up the road. By the time he pulled himself up to the road, he saw a green van rounding the distant curve. Overcome with exhaustion, pain and disappointment, he dropped against the ground, his chest heaving. He lay there a few minutes, then climbed the rest of the way up and dusted himself off.

A faded wooden sign by the side of the road announced that the Thief Creek Bed and Breakfast was one mile ahead.

Seven

The green van pulled to a dusty stop in the small parking lot in front of the inn. Before he opened his door, Tuffy Cribb, stuffed a fresh wad of chew in his cheek. He hopped out of the driver side onto the ground. The bandy-legged, fireplug of a wrangler, barely five feet tall, crossed to the other side of the van and slid open the passenger door with the Double J Ranch brand on it. He tugged the grimy brim of his battered felt Stetson firmly down on his forehead as he crossed the yard, then clumped up the wooden steps of the old log house.

He knocked on the screen door and called, "Hello? Mike? Miss Annie?"

Mike appeared at the front door and held it open for the cowboy. "Morning, Tuffy. Come on in. Steve and Heather will be down in a minute."

Tuffy dragged his scuffed old boots across the scraper bolted next to the door. He pushed his hat up with a thumb and smiled, unselfconscious about the mouthful of missing teeth, victims of various past rodeo and saloon events. "That's okay, Mike. I'll wait out here. You don't want me tracking critter poop on your floors. Beautiful day for a ride, ain't it?"

Mike scanned the bright blue sky. "Aren't they all?"

"You're right about that. I did hear on the radio on the way up that we might get a touch of rain this afternoon, though. Looked kind of cloudy down to the south on the other side of the valley. We could use the precip, that's for sure."

"Well, I hope it holds off till after the kids' ride."

"I think we'll be okay. It may blow off to the east before it reaches us in the mountains." He shrugged, "If we get rained out we'll take your guests on a ride tomorrow. How's Miss Annie doing?"

"She's fine. She's in Lame Elk at the clinic today."

Tuffy nodded. "Say, did you hear anything about the big doings down in Lame Elk?"

Mike shook his head. "No, I've been busy with breakfast. Why? What's up?"

"Don't know, but there were state troopers and the sheriff's car all around the Gas-N-Go when I drove by. I reckoned it might have something to do with those boys who escaped from Deer Lodge I heard about on the radio."

"What boys?" Mike asked. The two guests came up behind him before he got his answer.

"We're ready to go," said the woman brightly.

"Howdy, folks." Tuffy touched the brim of his hat and nodded toward the couple. He checked them out as he always did when he had new riders. They were both wearing blue jeans and T-shirts. That would work. She was wearing a brand new straw cowboy hat—a Shady Brady, he figured. Standard dude wear but looked dandy on her. Running shoes for her. Not great, but okay. Sandals and a New York Yankees cap on the husband. *Yankees*? He spat a little missile of brown tobacco juice into the dust. *Dudes*, he thought and shook his head with a grin hidden by the brim of his hat.

He looked up and said, "Looks like you folks are about ready to saddle up. I like you're hat, ma'am." That wasn't all he admired. The wife was a real looker. The boys at the Double J would be jealous as hell.

"Thank you," she snugged the hat down, grinned and held out her hand. "I'm Heather."

"Tuffy," he replied shaking her hand.

"I'm Steve," said the husband.

"Nice to meet you, sir." He shook Steve's hand then pointed at his cap. Without breaking a smile, he asked, "Is that a baseball team?"

Steve's face twisted quizzically, and he pulled the cap off to check it. "Yeah, it's the Yankees."

Tuffy nodded thoughtfully and snuck a brief wink at Mike. "Yankees, huh? They're a New York team ain't they? You folks from New York?"

"No, we're from Ohio," Steve answered. "I just like the Yankees."

"I see. Well, that's good, cause the horses at the Double J always seem to get a little ornery when they're rid by New Yorkers. You folks ever ride before?"

The two shook their heads in unison.

Staring down at Steve's feet, Tuffy scratched at the stubble on his jaw and pushed the brim of his hat back as if he was trying to solve the riddle of the ages. "I'm thinking you might want something on your feet besides those sandals. You got a pair of boots or even some sneakers?"

"I've got some hiking boots inside. Give me a second, and I'll go change." Steve bounded back in the house.

Tuffy sneaked another leathery-faced wink at Mike then turned to Heather. "Ma'am," he said. He offered his hand to Heather and escorted her to the van. Even with the high crown of his dusty Stetson, he was no taller than her shoulders. Steve came running out the door with his boots and socks in his hands as Tuffy helped his wife into the back seat.

The cowboy slid the door closed, climbed into the driver's seat and cranked the engine. Leaning out the side window, he waved as he backed up. "Have a good one, Mike. We should be back by dark thirty. Give my regards to Miss Annie."

He circled around the drive and turned back down Thief Creek Road.

EIGHT

Mike finished washing the last of the dishes and headed toward the stairs to make up the guest room when the phone rang. "Thief Creek Inn," he answered.

"Hi, honey." He could tell Annie was on her cell phone from the scratchy reception. "Are you done with breakfast?"

"All done and finished with the dishes. Nice couple of kids. They just left to go riding with Tuffy."

"I hope they have good weather. It was pouring rain down here. It looked like it was heading up your way. I just wanted—" The phone crackled. He didn't understand why she insisted on using that damn cell phone. There was no reception available at the inn, and even in town, the signal was iffy at best. One of the very few drawbacks of living in the mountains.

"... know I may be a little late tonight. It's been crazy around here. They brought that guy from the Gas-N-Go in this morning, but he was DOA."

"What guy?"

"Didn't you hear about the robbery? I guess you wouldn't if you were doing breakfast. The sheriff . . . men . . . all over . . ." Another broken sentence interspersed with static. Then the line went dead. Mike shook his head and sighed.

"Annie? Hello?" Mike punched in the number of the nurse's station at the clinic. He preferred to talk to her on a regular land line. No dial tone. He tried again, but the line was silent. *Great*, he thought. *The phone lines must be down again.* He shrugged and placed the phone back in its cradle. Technology was not always dependable where they were, and you either lived with it or moved into town.

Mike walked to the south facing window in the Sunroom. If rain was headed toward the inn, he'd need to close the windows upstairs. Despite the warm morning sun heating the room, he saw a dark cloud making its way across the valley. The misty curtain below it meant the rain would be upon them within thirty minutes or so. He recalled how tired they used to get of the perpetual rain back in Seattle. Now, in this semi-arid climate, the rain was a welcome blessing. The thunder and lightning could be so dramatic. Storms never lasted long enough for him.

He climbed the stairs and went from room to room closing the windows. The newlyweds' room looked like a tornado had hit it. Heather's suitcase was open on the floor with clothing erupting over its sides. Her running clothes were piled on the floor next to the bed. The sheets and comforter were twisted and hanging off the mattress in a heap along with the pillows. Steve's sandals were flung onto a chair that was also draped with his blue hospital scrubs shirt. The suitcase would be up to the kids to take care of, but the bed was his responsibility. He straightened out the sheets and made the bed. He fluffed the pillows. A noise from downstairs caused him to stop and listen. He thought he heard footsteps on the front porch.

Harsh rapping at the screen door told him he had a visitor.

It was uncommon to get drop-ins at the inn. In fact, the only unscheduled visitors they might get would be the FedEx man or the meter reader, and it was late in the morning for either of them. Besides, they rarely knocked. Occasionally, a lost fisherman or hunter might stop by for directions. It wasn't like Thief Creek Road was a well-traveled thoroughfare. The level of urgency that the insistent pounding on the door conveyed suggested it was none of the above. Mike glanced out the second story window to see if there was a truck or a car outside. Nothing. He quickened his step to the stairs to see who was there.

The man had let himself in and was standing in the entranceway when Mike came down. He was big and rough looking. His clothes were smudged with dirt as were his hands and face. A nasty lump on his forehead looked like it must be painful. Mike was shocked to see he was missing an ear, and he felt a quiet internal alarm quicken his heartbeat and heighten his senses. He put on his innkeeper smile and greeted his visitor. "Good morning. Can I help you?"

"Yeah, there's been an accident. I need help." The man's gruff voice did not allay Mike's sense of caution, but the desperation in his voice and his disheveled appearance shifted his emotions to concern and eagerness to assist.

"Our car flipped off the road about a mile from here, and my brother is badly hurt. I need to get him. Can I borrow your truck?" The man jabbed his thumb toward Mike's old Chevy pickup parked with its hood up near the shed.

"I'm sorry. My truck's not working. How badly is your brother hurt?"

The man glowered in thought. "Shit. Is there anyone around here with a car?

"Gee, no. The closest house is several miles from here. Let me see if I can call an ambulance. My phone's been kind of hinky this morning, but maybe it's working now."

The man's eyes narrowed in angry frustration. "We ain't got time for that. If you help me get him up here, we can maybe fix him up."

The guy's pushy attitude was off-putting, but Mike extended his hand. "My name is Mike, by the way."

The man stared at his hand and seemed confused, then shook it and mumbled, "Yeah."

"I have a four-wheeler. We can drive down there and bring him back up. My wife's a nurse, and we've got some pretty good first aid supplies. But if he's really hurt I'd better try to get someone up here. Just give me a minute."

"Well, hurry the fuck up," the man snapped.

The warning bells went off again in Mike's head, but he didn't have time to dwell on it. *The man was just upset about his brother.*

He picked up the phone and pressed the pre-programmed 911 button. The phone was still dead. "Damn it." He slammed the receiver down and grabbed the keys to his four-wheeler.

"No good on the phone. It's dead," he said and headed out past the man. "I'll get my four-wheeler. Hang on." On his way to the shed, Mike looked up at the darkening sky. They were going to get some rain for sure. And soon.

The ATV was a two-seater Bombardier Outlander Max 800. His ever-the-optimist father-in-law had bought it for him hoping he could convince Mike to go hunting with him when he visited. The thing was a monster and could easily handle two riders. He peeled the cover off and climbed on board. He had not ridden it since last fall, so he checked the gas gauge. There was less than a quarter tank, but enough to get them down the road and back. The engine roared awake when he hit the starter. He backed, swung around, and drove to the front of the inn where the man was standing and climbed off.

"I'll be right back," he said and ran in the house. He emerged moments later wearing a rain slicker and carrying a large case with a Red Cross decal on the front.

"Hop on," he said.

The man climbed onto the passenger seat as he strapped the first aid kit to the front rack.

As Mike maneuvered himself into the driver's seat, a jagged spear of lightning stabbed the distant crest of Elk Peak, and the first few drops of rain plopped onto the dusty top of the gas tank. Mike clicked the gear shift, twisted the throttle, and they tore out of the driveway with the big tires spitting pebbles and dirt behind them.

NINE

By the time they reached the spot where the car had left the road, the rain picked up. Jagged spikes of lightning sliced through the gray sky above the distant mountain tops. Mike pulled the hood of his slicker over his head and dismounted. He walked to the edge of the drop-off and peered down. A badly beat-up red Mustang leaned against a cottonwood about thirty feet down the gulch. Three men huddled together on the ground with their backs against the car. The one in the middle was being held by a huge shirtless man and appeared to be unconscious, asleep or dead.

"Holy crap," said Mike as the earless man came up next to him. "You guys are lucky to be alive. Are the other two okay?"

"Far as I know."

"What's your brother's name?"

Earless hesitated, then said, "Tom."

"It's going to be tough getting him up this slope. Can Tom walk?"

"Hell no, he can't walk. I told you he's badly wound . . . hurt. Let's get down there and get him up."

Mike clenched his jaw. Hurt brother or not, this guy's attitude was starting to get under his skin. The road at this spot was narrow. He couldn't leave the four-wheeler here. There was a slight ditch and some cottonwood trees across the road, so he maneuvered the ATV down into the ditch behind a fallen limb. He went to the front of the four-wheeler and yanked at the bungee cords securing the first aid kit. As he popped them free, he saw the earless guy start clambering down the rocks. He lifted the aluminum case and followed over the edge.

     Jeremy Soldevilla

The rain pelted down harder, making the already slippery apron of loose shale even more difficult to maneuver. Trying not to lose the cumbersome case, Mike slipped and skidded his way down the scree using his free hand to steady himself each time the rocks gave way under his feet.

By the time he reached the accident site, the rain came down full force and turned to white beads of sleet that pinged off the sides of the car and stung his hands and face.

One of the men stood and joined Earless who was bent over the one called Tom. The shirtless one was cradling Tom and pressing a bloody shirt against his back. The wounded man was unconscious and as pale as the sleet landing and melting on his face. Mike hurried over with the first aid kit and knelt next to Earless. He placed the kit on the ground just as the wind roared through the gully like a freight train. The clamoring assault of the sleet and wind was deafening, and he had to yell to be heard even though he was only inches away from the man's good ear. "What happened to him?"

The big man and the standing one exchanged concerned looks.

"Who is this guy, Jesse?" the big one yelled. It looked like he had badly split his lip, but didn't seem to be bleeding.

Jesse said, "Name's Mike. From up at the B and B. He's got a first aid kit. We're going to get Tommy out of here." Addressing the other one, he said, "JP, you okay?"

The one named JP had a laceration on his forehead that was still bleeding, but not too bad. He fingered the top of his head gingerly and said, "Yeah. I'll live. How do you figure we're going to get him up that hill?"

The four of them turned and surveyed the intimidating wall of broken rock behind them.

"Hell if I know," Jesse snapped back. "But we're going to fucking do it."

"Jesse. Is that your name? Jesse?" Mike yelled. Earless glowered at him without answering. The piercing sleet storm and Jesse's intractability made Mike shiver with a mixture of cold and anger. "I've got a fifty foot winch cable on my four-wheeler. We can fashion a stretcher out of my slicker and haul him up with that. " Jesse stuck his bottom lip out and nodded as he contemplated the idea.

"But first," Mike continued and unsnapped the lid of the first aid kit, "we need to take a look at his back. What happened?"

Again, the men exchanged nervous looks.

"I don't know," Jesse finally said. "I guess when we tumbled down the mountain something in the car stuck him. A pipe or something. I don't know. It don't matter. We just got to get him out of here."

Kneeling next to the wounded man, Mike opened the first aid kit doing his best to keep it protected from the weather by sliding it under the car. He pulled a wad of cotton out of the case and turned to the big man. "What's your name?"

The man glanced up at Jesse who nodded back."Butch."

At first, Mike thought Butch had badly damaged his mouth in the accident. His lip was split up to his nose, but there was no blood. Upon closer inspection, Mike realized that the split lip was not due to the accident, but that the man had a bad harelip. "Butch, I've got to take a look here." Mike carefully pulled the sodden shirt from the boy's back. Tom moaned quietly from his unconscious sleep. As soon as the shirt plug came away from the wound, blood burbled out in a stream, mixing with the rain and sleet. He dabbed at it with a large cotton ball. The wound was neat and circular. He'd seen this kind of hole before—in the sides of the deer that his father-in-law had shot on the hunting trip he had accompanied him on. What was the likelihood that a pipe would have pierced his side in the accident? What pipe?

Without thinking, Mike mumbled to himself, "This looks like a bullet wound." As he spoke the words, his brain played back the snippets of news he'd heard today from Annie and Tuffy. " . . . Robbery at the Gas-n-Go . . . DOA . . . Sheriff . . . boys who escaped from Deer Lodge . . . "

"What did you say?" Jesse called above the pelting sleet.

Mike eyed the three men standing over him. Each was grimacing and bracing himself against the nasty weather that beat down on them, their similar red hair plastered to their faces. The same uncomfortable feeling he had felt when he first met Jesse crept over him now, even more intensely. The icy wind whipped their wet clothes. A sharp gust blew the tail of Jesse's shirt up enough to reveal a gun butt stuck in the top of his pants. Mike's eyes widened involuntarily. His pulse quickened, and he felt like someone had pulled a stopper out of the base of his stomach. A chill, as if ice water had been poured down his spine, gripped him and shook his entire body. It wasn't from the sleet.

He lifted his eyes to Jesse's, praying that he hadn't noticed that he'd seen the gun butt. He raised his voice above the wind, trying to keep the quiver out of it. "I said this wound looks bad. He needs a doctor."

Jesse yelled back, "Right. But we don't have one, do we? Let's get him back to your place and take it from there."

"Sure," said Mike. "Help me get this bandage around him, and we'll haul him up." The big one, Butch, bent and held Tom steady as Jesse and Mike plugged the wound and bandaged him up as well as they could.

The wind howled around them, and the sleet returned to a driving rain. Despite the nastiness of the weather, Mike peeled out of his raincoat and handed it to Jesse. "Here. Wrap this around Tom and make it into a stretcher that we can pull him up this hill with. I've got some rope on my four-wheeler we can rig up to the winch cable, so just make sure he's secure in that slicker."

Jesse and Butch both nodded and bent to their task. The one called JP stood above them with his arms wrapped around himself huddled against the storm.

Mike began the tricky climb up the scree, slipping and slicing his hands against the teeth-like shards of rock. He made his way up the hill, hunched against the buffeting wind. As he crawled on all fours, slowly making progress, he considered his situation. There was little reason for these men to be on Thief Creek Road. The B and B was the only building up this way. They certainly weren't headed to the Inn. Beyond that, the road became little more than a rocky cow path leading into the National Forest Service land. Anyone trying to traverse that area would need a four-wheel drive vehicle, not a shiny red Mustang. They didn't appear to be hikers. Maybe they were there to fish, but if that was the case, why was Jesse packing a pistol? It wasn't unusual for back country travelers to carry a gun for protection against snakes and other animals, but it was unusual to stick the gun in your pants rather than in a holster.

Then there was the wounded man, Tom. That sure looked like a bullet wound in his back. If it was, why would Jesse lie about it? It could have been an accident. If it wasn't, though, if someone shot him intentionally . . . Were these the men involved in the robbery in Lame Elk? There was nothing pleasant about any of them.

A loud crash of thunder cracked across the mountain tops, and Mike flattened himself against the side of the hill, his heart pounding. He closed his eyes and breathed out, then restarted his climb.

What would he do when he got them to the inn? He couldn't make any phone calls, and he had no vehicle to get away in. Maybe he should just leave them down in the gully and make a run for it. Get to the Mickelson ranch and call for help there. But, no, there probably wasn't enough gas in the tank to get him there. He could drive back to the inn, get his shotgun and come back and get the drop on these guys.

Get the drop on them? Who am I kidding? What did he know about getting the drop on anyone? And how would he match up against those three desperate men, each of whom probably had his own gun?

Maybe he should just take off and hide out in the mountains. He gave a quick look over his shoulder back down at the men huddled and working over the boy. That kid was going to die if he didn't get help. The only one who could help him was Mike himself. *Think* he told himself. *What is the right thing to do? What would Annie tell me to do?* He knew what Annie would say. She'd make him bring the wounded man up and treat his wound. Save his life, and not worry about what the three other men would do until she had to cross that bridge. It was partially the nurse in her, but it was more the deep humanity and strength that was so much a part of her makeup.

He looked back again and saw that they had secured the wounded man and stood over him. Jesse gestured in his direction, and the big one named Butch started to follow his trail up the mountainside. *Great.* Barring a miracle, there wasn't much else he could do now but help the boy.

As he neared the top, he thought he heard a vehicle through the noise of the rain and wind. He doubled his efforts to reach the road to wave down whoever it was. Maybe this was the miracle he needed. He glanced over his shoulder and saw Butch gaining on him.

TEN

Tuffy leaned into the steering wheel as close as he could get to squint through the windshield of the van. He should have replaced the damn wipers after the last rain they'd had. Even new wiper blades would have been hard-pressed to deal with this downpour, but the ragged ones uselessly waving in front of him now provided no clarity of visibility. Fortunately, he knew Thief Creek Road well. Unfortunately, he knew it was a dangerous road even in the best of weather because of its switchbacks and narrow passages.

"It don't usually rain much out here," he said, trying to make conversation to soothe his nervous passengers. The couple also leaned forward in the back seat, intently keeping their eyes peeled to the windshield. "But this one's a frog floater. We can always use the rain, though. I'm sorry it halted the ride before we even got started. But, we'll get you out there tomorrow for sure. And you'll see that this rain will have made everything even more beautiful along the trail. Bluebells, red Indian Paint Brush and bright yellow Black-eyed Susans. You'll see."

"Sounds nice," Stephen commented quietly from the backseat. Glancing at the young doctor's strained face in the rearview mirror, the wrangler could tell he was more focused on what he could see of the road ahead than the colorful picture Tuffy was trying to paint.

"Don't worry, folks, we're almost there. Only about a mile more."

Up ahead Tuffy could just make out a red four-wheeler parked off the road.

He glanced at the ATV on the side of the road and shook his head. "Look at that. Some poor bastard got stuck out here on his four-wheeler in this rain. He probably hunkered down under some trees. I hope it ain't Mike. We haven't had a good storm like this all year."

The van splashed up into the driveway of the Thief Creek B and B and came to a halt at the inn's entrance.

"Here we are." Tuffy jumped out and ran around to the passenger side. Sliding the door open, he offered a hand to Heather who took it and hopped down. Steve followed behind, and the two ran up the steps of the front porch out of the downpour.

"Sorry about the rain today," Tuffy said and peered down toward the valley. Beyond the gray clouds, he saw bright sunshine and blue sky making its way toward the mountains. "It actually looks like it might clear up soon. But the trails would still be a might muddy. I'll come by to pick you up tomorrow at the same time, and we'll have a nice ride. I promise."

Heather waved from the porch. "It was nice meeting you, Tuffy. We'll see you in the morning."

The wrangler tugged the brim of his weathered Stetson and drew himself up into the driver's seat. He shot a wad of tobacco out the window, then circled the van out on to the road.

Steve and Heather entered the inn and called out for Mike. They searched the common areas, but he was nowhere to be seen.

"Looks like he's not here," said Steve.

Heather hugged Steve's arm and rested her head on his shoulder. "That must have been Mike's four-wheeler that we passed on the road. So, that means we've got the place to ourselves. If the rain lets up, do you want to join me in the hot tub down in the trees?" She took his ear lobe between her teeth and pulled gently. She felt the electricity spark instantly between them.

Steve moaned and closed his eyes.

Heather breathed into his ear and whispered teasingly, "We don't have to wear anything."

"I would love to get in the hot tub with you."

She probed the inner part of his ear with the tip of her tongue. "Really?" she sighed blowing her warm breath across his neck.

"God, yes." Steve's voice quivered.

Heather ran her lips up the side of Steve's neck and whispered, "You only have to do one little thing for me first, though. Okay?" She ran her hand down the front of his shirt and squeezed the bulge in his pants.

"Whatever you want. Anything."

"Promise?" she squeezed again.

Steve's breathing was coming heavier. "Jesus, Heather. Yes, I promise. Whatever you want. You're driving me crazy."

"Okay, let's go for a quick run first."

Steve stepped back with an incredulous look on his face. Heather giggled. "What? You want to go for a run first? In this rain?"

She nodded vigorously, her blonde curls bouncing around her face.

"You're crazy." he said.

She nodded again, then gave him the pouty little girl face that she knew always did him in. "You promised. And you told me this morning you'd run with me later. Look." she pointed to the lightening sky. "It's already starting to clear up. We'll just take a quick run and then jump right in the hot tub. And afterward, you, Doctor Steve, can give me a thorough medical examination."

Steve gave a dramatic sigh and rolled his eyes. "All right. A short run. But you, Ms. Physical Trainer, will have to help me exercise my muscles when we get back."

"My pleasure, Doctor." She winked at him and dashed up the stairs to change with her husband following close behind.

By the time they finished their run, the rain stopped and was replaced by a warm Montana afternoon sun. Sparkling droplets hung like thousands of tiny diamonds from the tips of the dark green needles of the pine trees. As Tuffy had predicted, the mountainsides were awash in brilliant flowers of many colors. Bluebirds flitted and sang along the fence tops, and black and white magpies flew their jagged patterns across the sky.

The sun and fresh mountain air felt like a tonic to the newlyweds as they ran down to the stand of trees where the hot tub sat. The cedar tub was surrounded on three sides by tall lodgepole pines. The side facing the inn was exposed to the back yard, but still fairly well concealed. Below it, a well-traveled game trail showed evidence of the deer, elk and moose that traversed it on their way to the creek. A crude shower stall had been set up nearby and sported a sign asking guests to rinse off before and after entering the tub.

Heather pulled off her sweaty running clothes and jumped into the shower. Steve looked up at the inn before stripping down. "What if Mike can see us?" he said.

"Don't be such a prude," Heather chided him. "There's no one up there. Get in here."

Steve squinted up at the inn again, then quickly undressed and joined his wife in the cramped stall.

"Last one in's a rotten egg," Heather said shutting off the water. She dashed from the shower to the hot tub. She flipped a switch, and the surface of the blue water began to bubble like a volcano. Translucent plumes of steam wafted up and disappeared in the shadowy canopy of firs.

From the doorway of the shower, Steve watched her every move. She looked like some beautiful naked wood nymph mystically surrounded by clouds of mist, her long graceful leg stretched out to test the water. Shafts of sunlight pierced the branches, creating a halo of golden highlights in her hair. *How did I get so lucky*, he wondered. Her body was perfect. Tight and firm everywhere; not an ounce of fat. He had to admit he felt a little jealous when he saw other men ogling her. A little pride, but a little jealousy at the same time.

Steve had grown up in a conservative Midwestern family. His father was a minister in a small farming community, and his mother was the good minister's good wife. His parents subscribed to a stiff moral code and brought their son and his sister up feeling uncomfortable about exposing their nakedness. A bold new world opened up to Steve when he moved to Columbus to attend Ohio State. Much of it was opened by the pretty coed in his organic chemistry class.

Heather seemed to have no inhibitions whatsoever. Where he was shy and studious, preferring his textbooks to socializing, she was gregarious and full of energy and life. He had few friends. Heather, on the other hand, could be dropped into a roomful of strangers and by the end of the evening be laughing and the center of attention, introducing each one to him by name. He was happy to spend his weekends in the biology lab, while she insisted that they get out and go hiking, cycling, swimming or jogging. She exhausted him, but he loved her for it. And she seemed to enjoy being the alpha partner.

He recalled one time in a hangout back in college where he and some of their friends had gotten together for the evening. It had been a long day prepping for his upcoming exams, and he was tired. Heather, however, was her usual hyperkinetic self, having just aced her self-defense instructor certification that afternoon. One of the over-developed gym rats from her club and three of his over-served buddies had been leering at her from the bar all night. When she got up to go the ladies room, the muscle-head greeted her as she passed by them. She acknowledged him with a brief smile and walked on. Steve watched as the gang of four made lewd hand signals and cat-calls behind her back. When Heather returned from the bathroom, the big guy downed his beer, swung his beefy arm around her and pulled her against him offering to buy her a drink. Steve's fist clenched, but his legs felt like Jell-O. He'd had too many margaritas and was totally outmatched by the boorish creep, let alone his buffed-up friends. But his sense of chivalry demanded that he defend his fiancée. He hesitated, trying to decide what to do.

In retrospect, Heather might have overreacted, but she was pumped and maybe a little drunk herself. Steve watched wide-eyed as if in slow motion, she reached across with her left hand and removed the gorilla's grip from her side. In the same move, her other arm swung up and over his thick neck. A quick upward yank of his arm and a sharp opposing downward twist of his neck brought the bewildered behemoth crashing to the floor. His shocked friends leapt back, their barstools thudding behind them in unison.

As if she had just done nothing more than put a pan of cookies in the oven, Heather brushed her hands together, smiled, stepped over the dazed drunk and said, "No thank you. I have a drink." She returned to the table amidst a standing ovation from the bar patrons. You had to love a woman like that.

It had been her idea to honeymoon in Montana. He had suggested New York with its Broadway shows, fancy restaurants and big city excitement. But Heather had her heart set on experiencing the wild and untamed landscape of what the brochures called "The Last Best Place." She spent weeks searching the net for ideas. Her enthusiasm for their trip to Montana eclipsed even her former excitement about planning the wedding. Horseback riding, whitewater rafting, rock climbing, mountain biking, Glacier National Park, Yellowstone. Every time she emailed another recreation site to Steve, he got more exhausted. He loved her boundless energy and wished that he had some himself. However, after the long hours and stress of being an intern, he just wanted a rest. He was relieved that she finally settled on a quiet bed and breakfast high up in the Rocky Mountains that would enable him to relax and refresh himself.

So, here they were in Montana. He had to admit it was even more breathtaking than he had expected. A far cry from the flat landscape of Ohio.

Steve peeked around the shower stall toward the inn. A cool breeze whispered up from the creek, and he huddled in the opening, covering himself.

"What are you doing?" Heather called as she slid into the steaming spa. "Are you cold? Come on in here. It's hot."

Steve gave her a weak smile. "I'm just going to go and make sure no one's up at the inn checking us out and get us some robes. Do you want anything?"

"A glass of wine and some grapes would be wonderful."

"Wine? It's not even 2:00."

Heather tilted her head and frowned at him playfully. "Hello? It's our honeymoon. Remember? I'm naked in a hot tub. I want some wine. And you. Any other questions, dummy?"

Just then, the giant white cloud that was meandering across the sky passed overhead revealing the sun. Brilliant, blinding brightness washed over the mountains and the timber. A shaft of golden light bathed Heather in a full body halo as if it was her own inner radiance that was illuminating the space around her.

Steve swallowed at the sight of her. "Okay, wine it is," he said. "I'll be right back."

Heather wiggled her fingers at him, then, holding her nose, dunked herself under the surface of the bubbling waters.

Still crouching in his nakedness, Steve sprinted up to the inn, praying that no one was there.

ELEVEN

Mike was almost to the top of the hill when he heard the vehicle above splashing and bumping up the road. With a look over his shoulder and renewed effort, he scuttled up the last ten feet of the climb. Butch had shortened the distance between them and was coming on doggedly.

He pulled himself up and over the top of the hill in time to see the green van with the horse heads on the back plowing past and up the road toward the inn. *Tuffy*, he thought. A quick look down the gully told him he had enough time to wave at the retreating van before Butch would reach him. He stepped into the middle of the road to avoid being seen from below and waved madly with both arms. *Please let me see those brake lights.* The van kept bouncing its way up the mountain. He slowly dropped his arms, and his shoulders sagged as the van disappeared around the next switchback turn.

Rocks tumbled down the hill behind him, and he heard the grunting and cursing of Butch bulling his way up to the road. Once he crested the top, he bent over and rested with his lacerated hands on his knees trying to catch his breath. Mike was amazed at the huge muscles on the man. He wasn't a young man. Judging by the gray mixed in with his short-cropped red hair, Mike figured him to be close to his own age, maybe older, but in much better physical shape. His biceps were as big as Mike's thighs. His massive pecs and sculpted abs bulged threateningly. Tattoos of all sorts and colors decorated his arms, chest, neck and back. As he straightened up and Mike got a look at his face, he presented a terrifying spectacle with his monster's body, his bleeding hands, and most horrifying, his crooked harelip that split up to his nose.

"Jesse told me to give you a hand," the monster growled between wheezing breaths.

Mike's mind was spinning. Tuffy would be coming back shortly after dropping off the kids at the inn. If he could get rid of Butch, he could flag down Tuffy and race down to somewhere he could contact the sheriff. It might work. But what about Steve and Heather? These thugs could make their way up to the inn and harm them or hold them hostage or something. What the hell, though. Tuffy might be his only chance.

"What do you want me to do?" Butch said with a touch of impatience.

"Come with me," Mike said. The two crossed the road to where he had parked the four-wheeler. Mike opened a supply case and extracted a coil of rope. He handed it to Butch and told him to take it down to the car and secure it around Tom so they could pull him up.

Butch accepted the rope and started for the edge. Then he stopped and turned. "You coming?"

"I'll be down in a minute with the winch cable. I need to strap the four-wheeler off to one of these trees to make sure we don't pull it down on top of us. You go ahead."

Butch paused and peered for a moment over the edge at the men below. "I'll wait for you. My brother told me to stick with you."

The sinking feeling in Mike's gut returned. "So, you are all brothers," he said trying to formulate a plan.

"Yeah. Brothers. Why?"

"Nothing. I was just trying to figure out what you fellows were doing up here on Thief Creek Road."

Butch's eyes narrowed. "You don't have to worry about that right now. Let's get going."

"Look, Butch. Right? Your name is Butch?"

Butch neither answered nor nodded.

"We don't have a lot of time. It's going to take you a while to get Tom ready, and I need to swing my four-wheeler around and strap it to those trees. Just head down there, and I'll be along as soon as I secure the ATV." He pointed to a stand of aspens growing just before where the Mustang had plunged off the road.

Butch hesitated, giving it some thought. "All right, but hurry up."

Mike felt his chest relax as he watched Butch climb over the edge. "Okay. I'll be down in a minute." He looked up the road hoping to see the Double J van returning to rescue him. No van, but at least the rain was starting to ease up.

He mounted the four-wheeler, started it and swung it across the road. He parked it tight against the thickest aspen trunk. Retrieving a yellow tow strap from the supply case, he lashed the four-wheeler to the tree, keeping an eye on the road for Tuffy. He heard rocks sliding as Butch worked his way down the mountainside. Taking his time, he unlatched the winch cable on the front of his ATV.

"Hey, hurry up," Butch called.

"Be right there," Mike yelled down.

As he extended the winch cable, he looked up and saw the green van turn round the curve in the road. His pulse quickened with excitement. Glancing to make sure Butch was occupied with his descent, Mike waved at the distant van. Tuffy responded with a double honk on the horn.

Shit, thought Mike. Did Butch hear that? He peered again over the edge and saw that Butch had thrown the rope aside and was scrambling with amazing speed like some giant crab back up the slope.

The sinking feeling in his gut returned with a vengeance. *Come on, Tuffy. Hurry up.* He looked anxiously from the van to Butch. He just might get lucky.

Tuffy pulled the van up on the far side of the road and hailed Mike. "Hey, partner, what the hell are you doing out in this rain?"

With a quick glance back, Mike approached the vehicle. "Tuffy, I need—"

Mike saw Tuffy lift his head and look over his shoulder. The wide-eyed expression of shocked surprise on the wrangler's face told Mike it was too late.

TWELVE

uffy stared at Butch, then back at Mike. His quizzical look told Mike he needed to come up with an explanation. But how was he going to explain this tattooed, broken-faced, shirtless giant?

Before he could think of an answer, Butch spoke from directly behind him, so close Mike could feel the heat from his breath on his ear. "Hey, brother. How're you doing?"

Mike watched Tuffy's eyes explore the big man. He shut his gaping mouth and gulped. "Uh, fine thanks. Mike, you boys okay?"

Butch clamped a friendly hand firmly down on Mike's shoulder and said, "Oh, we're fine. Mike and I were fishing in the creek below when the rain hit. We got drenched. We just climbed up to ride up to Mike's place to get a change of clothes. Right, Mike?"

A sharp pain cut into Mike as Butch dug his fingers into the nape of his neck. He forced a smile on his face and despite the cool weather felt a bead of sweat roll down his cheek. "That's right. Almost had a nice brookie on the line when the hail started pounding us. After we change, I'm going back to catch that bugger."

Tuffy looked from Mike to Butch, then back again. "Well, that's a shame. But there's plenty more where he came from. That's for sure. Yeah, that storm was something, huh? I had to bring your folks back it was raining so hard at the ranch. I told them we'd take them out tomorrow when things dried up." He lifted his chin toward Butch and said, "Who's your buddy?"

Mike's heart thumped against his chest in silent desperation. "Oh, sorry, this is . . . "

Butch stepped forward and stuck out a beefy hand. "Dan. Dan Johnson. Nice to meet you."

Tuffy's eyes shifted again from Butch to Mike and back, then he reached out and shook the proffered hand. "I'm Tuffy. Nice to meet you too, Dan. You staying up at the inn?"

"Yeah, just taking in the mountain scenery and spending a few days relaxing."

"Well, you're in the right place for that. Mike will take good care of you. If you're looking to go horseback riding, give us a call. Like I said, I'll be by tomorrow morning at ten to pick up Steve and Heather. You ought to come along too."

Butch smiled, the cleft below his nose spreading like an opening curtain.

Mike cringed inside at the hideous sight his deformed face made. A mixture of fear, frustration and anger churned in his stomach. *Why can't I say something? This is my only chance.* But the words wouldn't come.

"Thanks, Tuffy. I might take you up on that."

Tuffy gave a brief tug at the brim of his hat, then turned to Mike and said, "I'll let you boys get on your way. I've got to get back to the Double J. Too bad the rain didn't stop an hour ago. It's turning into a beautiful day." He put the truck in gear. "Have a good one, gentlemen."

The van slowly crunched along the gravel as Mike watched his only hope for rescue disappear down the road.

"You done real good," Butch said to Mike. "Now let's go get Tommy." He turned and headed toward the drop-off.

Halfway across the road Mike stopped and said, "I want to know what's going on here."

Butch turned and raised a quizzical eyebrow.

The mixture of fear and frustration Mike had felt before Tuffy left was turning to anger. He had a growing awareness of the possible danger he was in and felt the need to assert himself. "What was with the fake name and the bullshit fishing story?" he said.

The look of amused surprise on Butch's face countered the shock in his own mind that he was talking this way to this bull of a man.

Butch crossed the road and towered a good foot and a half above Mike. He dropped his two meaty paws on Mike's shoulders and looked deep into his eyes. The piss and vinegar Mike had felt a moment ago drained out of him.

"Friend," he said, "those are my brothers down there. My youngest brother is bleeding to death, and we need to get him taken care of. You're going to help us do that. And that's all you need to know right now." He continued to glare into Mike's eyes for a moment longer, then turned and took three steps, stopped and turned back.

"Oh, one more thing you need to know. If you try screwing with us?" he paused. "I promise I will kill you. Now get down there." He turned again and disappeared over the edge.

Mike exhaled, releasing some of the tension in his body, and followed Butch down the mountainside. But his heart beat against his chest like a jack hammer.

By the time they reached the car, Tommy's condition had worsened. His face was ashen and his body limp, his head lolled to one side. His brothers had trussed him up inside the slicker. and fashioned a travois out of some limbs from the cottonwood tree. Jesse moved him in position to hook the arrangement to the winch cable. He stood as Mike and Butch approached.

"What the hell were you doing up there?" he said, the last of a cigarette bobbing up and down in his mouth as he spoke.

Mike noticed that despite being much bigger and more threatening than his brother, Butch was deferential to Jesse.

"One of Mike's buddies was driving by and stopped to see what we were doing. I got rid of him though." Butch said with a touch of pride in his voice.

Jesse's eyes widened in disbelief. "What do you mean you got rid of him? Did you get his car for crissake?" He threw his spent cigarette on the ground.

Butch's brow furrowed, "No. I figured we should get rid of him as soon as possible. We don't need more trouble. Once we get Tommy patched up, we can take Mikey Boy's car from the inn."

Jesse's face turned red, and he fired a wad of spit on the ground. "You idiot. 'Mikey Boy' doesn't have a car. His truck is busted. Now we've got no way out of here."

Butch scuffed his foot in the dirt. "Hell, I didn't know. I didn't think—"

Jesse glared at his brother. "Yeah, that's just it. You didn't think." He shook his head then turned back toward Tommy. "Come on. Let's get him out of here."

JP and Butch joined Jesse at Tommy's side. They helped settle their wounded brother on the ground and secured the rope around the makeshift stretcher. Mike pulled the cable closer and fastened the other end of the rope to the winch hook. He said, "I think it's best if we carry him as much as possible. I'll go up and run the winch, and you guys steady the stretcher as we pull him up the rocks."

Butch looked at Jesse and said, "You want me to go with him?"

"No. The three of us need to maneuver Tommy up this hill. Mike won't take off on us, will you, Mike?"

His tone told Mike this was a rhetorical statement, not a question. He shook his head and began the rocky climb back up the scree.

As he made his way up the hillside, he tried to put his thoughts in order to come up with a plan. First and foremost, no matter what, he had to help the boy named Tommy. Regardless of who these men were or what they had done; it wasn't in his nature to abandon a dying man. Butch's chilling warning about not screwing with them echoed in his head. If he helped them with their brother, maybe they'd leave him alone until Annie got home. Then he could give them the van and let them escape. Surely, the phone service would be back by then, and he could call the sheriff and let him know what had occurred. He'd bargain the van for his and Annie's safety. He didn't want any trouble. He wasn't going to try any heroics. He had to laugh at himself. *Heroics? Right. I'm going to try to pull something with a thug with a gun and a giant tattooed gorilla with a harelip. I don't think so.*

But what about Steve and Heather? He'd forgotten about them. Tuffy had dropped them off at the inn. They'd soon be meeting the brothers, and now they would be in danger too. *Isn't Steve a doctor?* He remembered now that Steve had mentioned this at breakfast. He'd be able to help patch up Tommy; at this point, probably save his life. The kid didn't look good at all. So that was the plan—fix the kid up, wait for Annie, give them the van and let them get the hell out of there.If everybody just stayed cool, and that meant everybody, maybe they'd get through this okay. His foot lost its purchase on a loose rock, and he slid back opening a gash in the palm of his hand.

"Bastard!" he swore as a trickle of blood snaked down his wrist. *Yeah, stay cool*, he thought. *That's me. Always the optimist.*

THIRTEEN

Steve was relieved to see that Mike had not returned to the house yet. Despite the fact no one was in the inn, he still felt self-conscious about his nudity and dashed up to the bedroom to grab a couple of robes. After wrapping himself in one of them, he picked up the other and snatched the bottle of wine they'd bought yesterday. As he passed the window, he looked down on Heather who was luxuriating in the tub with her back facing the inn. He smiled and the old Joe Cocker song, *You Are So Beautiful*, floated into his head. A peaceful happiness and gratitude for such a wonderful person being in his life settled over him, and he hummed the tune as he descended the stairs.

Glasses, he thought. *We need some wine glasses.* He headed to the kitchen still humming to himself. The growl of a distant engine caused him to pause. Something was coming up the road. He pulled the robe more tightly around himself and crossed the floor of the Great Room. He peered out the window and saw Mike on a four-wheeler driving slowly toward the inn. Walking beside him were three other men holding on to a bundle of something strapped to the front of the ATV.

The men with Mike looked rough, and one of them, the big one, was shirtless and covered with tattoos. His eyes widened as he finally made out what they were holding on to. It was a man lashed to the front of the four-wheeler.

He set the wine bottle and robe on the couch and ran to the front door.

"Mike!" he called and stepped out on to the porch letting the screen door slam behind him.

All four men looked up suddenly. One of them stepped aside, reached inside his shirt and pulled a pistol out and pointed it at him.

The four-wheeler stopped, and Mike gasped at the man holding the gun. "What the hell do you think you are doing?"

The man shoved the gun back in his pants. Without taking his eyes off Steve, he said, "He startled me. Who are you?"

For a moment, Steve was speechless. He looked from the gunman to Mike and then the man on the four-wheeler who was clearly in bad shape. He was unconscious but moaning, and his face was drained of blood. As if a button had been pushed, Steve's medical instincts took over. "I'm Doctor Kimble. What's wrong with this man?

"You're a doctor?" the gunman said.

"That's right," Steve answered. "What's wrong with him?" He approached the wounded man, glancing at each of the four men around the ATV as he crossed the yard.

"We had an acci—" the one with the gun began.

"He's been shot," Mike said. His tone was impatient and challenging.

"Shot?" said Steve. He looked at each man's face hoping for an explanation. He noticed Mike glaring at the one with the gun. The three other men looked from one to the other in a way that made Steve's pulse beat faster.

"I'm sorry about this," Mike said. "But we're going to need your help with this man."

Steve felt some of his professional composure slip away. His residency had been in family medicine. Removing a bullet wasn't on the syllabus, nor had he ever operated on someone as mortally wounded as the fellow on the stretcher appeared to be. "This man needs to get to a hospital. And fast."

"We have no car, Steve," Mike said. His voice was calm, and in sharp contrast to the increasing panic, Steve was feeling.

"Well, call 911."

"Can't," said Mike. "The phone is dead. At least, it was earlier. Besides, an ambulance couldn't make it up here from Lame Elk fast enough."

Steve glanced at the wounded man on the blood-drenched stretcher and knew Mike was right. His tongue stuck to the roof of his dry mouth. He gulped and took a deep breath. "Let's get him inside so I can get a look at him," Steve said focusing on the patient and avoiding anyone else's eyes. He hoped they didn't notice the tremor in his voice. "Mike, try the phone again. At least we can get some help on its way."

The man with the gun stepped over to him and glared into his eyes."Look, the phone is dead. The line's been cut. There ain't going to be no help. If you're a doctor, it's up to you. Understand?"

Steve gulped again and nodded.

Mike said, "How do you know the line's been cut?"

The gunman turned to Mike. "Because I cut it when I first came up here. Now quit gabbing and let's get on with this."

Mike stood with his mouth agape. It looked to Steve like he wanted to say something, but instead, he shook his head then moved to the ATV. Taking care not to jostle him, Mike and the other three men carefully lifted the fellow from the four-wheeler and carried him into the inn.

"There's a medical kit on the back of the four-wheeler," said Mike. "Grab that, and we'll put him in the bedroom on the first floor."

Steve lifted the first aid case and hurried up the stairs to the inn. He held the screen door open. As the men shuffled by him with their load, he saw that Mike's jaw was set and he and the gunman's eyes were locked. The large shirtless one sported evil-looking tattoos over most of his upper body. His brutish face was marred with a deep and ugly cleft pallet that accentuated his malevolent appearance.

Heather, he thought and felt his knees tremble.

❧   ❧   ❧

"Open the door on the Lewis and Clark Room up on the right, and we'll put him in there," Mike nodded toward the first room down the hall.

Steve squeezed by the stretcher detail and swung the door open for them.

"Steve, take that quilt off the bed. Let me spread the slicker under Tom, and then lay him down," Mike instructed the brothers. They carefully held Tom while he untied the oversized raingear and positioned it on the bed. He was glad he had thought of it, as the inside of the slicker was already drenched with blood.

Steve inspected the contents of the first aid kit, then crossed to the bedside as they laid the wounded man on his side. Mike and the brothers winced in unison as he peeled away the blood-caked shirt from Tom's back. He was surprised to see Butch cover his eyes and turn away. Steve gently probed the hole with his fingers, and dark blood oozed down the boy's side. After inspecting the wound, he covered it with a fresh wad of cotton and gauze and asked Butch to apply some pressure to the bandage.

"I have a few things up in my bag that I'm going to need. I'll be right back." Steve turned and exited the room leaving a momentary vacuum of silence behind him.

Mike and Jesse remained staring at each other, sizing the other one up without speaking. Finally, Jesse said, "All right, you figured it out. It's a bullet wound."

Mike pointed at Jesse's waist. "From your gun?"

Jesse paused, glanced out the window and ran his hand through his hair. He looked back directly into Mike's eyes and held his gaze. "No."

"Look," said Mike. "I don't care what happened. I just want to do what we can for Tom."

"His name is Tommy," JP spoke for the first time. He was kneeling next to the bed and stroking the boy's head.

"I just want to do what we can for Tommy," Mike continued. "Then you guys can be on your way. I want you out of here."

Jesse took a menacing step toward Mike, stopping inches from his face. "And where are we going to go, Mike? Your truck's busted and we've got a wounded man here. What do you suggest we do?"

Jesse's breath was hot and foul, and Mike took a step back. Before he could respond, he heard Steve's footsteps from the hallway. He entered the room wearing his Yankees cap backwards and carrying a leather toilet kit. He crossed to the patient.

"Can you get me a couple of towels, Mike?" Steve asked. "And some alcohol."

Mike retrieved a hand towel and two bath towels from the bathroom.

Steve nodded thanks and asked him to put the hand towel on the nightstand next to the bed. He took the other towels and placed them alongside Tommy's body. He set the toilet kit down and removed a hemostat, a suturing needle, thread, a syringe, a small bottle and a scalpel. Mike noticed his hands were shaking as he placed the supplies on the towel.

Steve put the first aid kit on a nearby chair and took a package of cotton and gauze bandages from the bag. He laid them next to the other items on the nightstand. The Toomey brothers watched each move intently. The young doctor pulled on a pair of latex gloves and tied a surgical mask from his kit on his face. Mike could see he was breathing heavily as the mask drew in and out with each nervous breath. He wiped his forehead with his shirt sleeve, then examined the equipment on the nightstand.

"Alcohol," he shouted, causing everyone to start. "Where's the alcohol? Mike, I told you to get me some alcohol."

Mike, who had also been caught up in observing his every move, jumped at the sharp tone. "Oh, yeah. I'm sorry. I'll go check, I'm not sure we have any."

"It doesn't have to be rubbing alcohol. Do you have any whiskey? Scotch? Whatever."

"Sure. I'll get something," Mike said and hurried out of the room. He returned a moment later with a bottle of Jack Daniels. "Will this work?"

"Fine," said Steve, and wiped his forehead on his sleeve once more.

Jesse watched Steve closely and said, "You ever remove a bullet before, Doc?"

"I know what I'm doing," Steve snapped, his voice cracking slightly. Mike noticed he avoided making eye contact with Jesse as he said it. After a pause, he took a deep breath, turned to Jesse and said, "Look, I'll do what I can for your friend here . . . "

"He's our brother," JP said, still smoothing Tommy's hair.

Steve looked from face to face. "You're all brothers?" He took a deep breath. "Okay, I'm going to be honest with you. Your brother has lost a lot of blood and should really be in a hospital. I don't carry a lot of equipment with me, just a few essentials. I don't have any anesthetic."

"What's the syringe for?" asked Jesse.

"I'm going to give him a shot of antibiotic to fight infection. But I don't have anything to numb him. The alcohol will help a bit, but not much. Removing the bullet is going to be very painful. In his weakened condition, he could die from loss of blood or shock."

A curtain of silence dropped over the room. Mike watched a tear roll down JP's cheek.

Jesse cleared his throat and said in an even, firm tone, "There's no way we can get him to a hospital. You're going to have to do this, and you're not going to let him die."

Butch's massive arms were folded over his naked barrel chest, his fists clenched. "That's right. You'd better not let him die." Butch looked a little pale.

Another bead of sweat ran down Steve's forehead, and his eyes grew big above his surgical mask at the implied threat.

"Steve, what can I do to help?" Mike asked, breaking the silence that hung in the air.

Steve blinked, then focused his attention on Mike. "It's hot in here. I'll need you to wipe my forehead as I work so the sweat doesn't get in my eyes." It didn't feel particularly warm in the room to Mike, but he picked up the hand towel in preparation. "When I tell you, I want you to pour some of that whiskey right on the wound."

"Jesus," said Butch.

"He's going to scream," Steve continued. "You." He said pointing at JP.

"Name's JP."

"Get a washcloth from the bathroom, roll it tight and put it in Tommy's mouth for him to bite down on. Then I want you to hold his jaw firmly when he starts screaming. Can you do that, JP?"

JP nodded and headed to the bathroom.

"Oh God," said Butch.

Nodding at both Jesse and Butch, Steve said, "I'll need you two to hold him down. You, what's your name?"

"I'm Jesse and that's Butch."

"Jesse, you come over here. Butch, you take that side. He's going to start kicking. Do not let him move. Not an inch. Got it?"

Jesse came around the side of the bed and said, "I got it."

Steve nodded at Butch. "Not an inch. You understand, Butch?"

Butch took his position without saying anything. The blood had drained out of his face and his eyes were wild. It looked to Mike like he might pass out at any moment. *For such a big tough guy, he's not taking this very well*, he thought.

It seemed Steve, too, had observed Butch's trepidation. "You going to be okay, Butch?" he asked.

"Shut up and let's get this over with," Butch growled.

JP put the rolled washcloth between Tommy's teeth and placed his hands on the boy's jaw and head.

"Everybody ready?" Steve looked from one member of his shaky team to the other.

"Hold on," said Jesse turning to Mike. "Is there anyone else staying here?"

Steve shot a frightened glance at Mike.

"Uh, no," said Mike looking back in Steve's eyes. He wondered where Heather was and hoped she stayed out of the room. Steve returned his gaze with a look of nervous gratitude.

"All right, Doc," said Jesse adjusting his grip, "Let's get the show on the road."

Steve wiped his brow on his sleeve and took a deep breath, then exhaled. A large stain of perspiration already soaked his cap. Using the hemostat, he carefully peeled back the temporary bandage and dropped it on the nightstand. The skin around the wound had become puffy and dark flakes of dried blood were encrusted around the opening. "Mike, mop me, and get ready with the alcohol."

Mike dabbed at the doctor's forehead and picked up the bottle of Jack Daniels.

"Okay," said Steve with a slight tremble in his voice. "Let's do this." He opened the hemostat and held it ready. The three brothers braced their holds on Tommy.

"Mike. Alcohol."

With shaking hands, Mike poured a generous amount of the whiskey into the wound. Dark red blood and brown whiskey burbled from the hole. Tommy's eyes flew open and his body arched. JP held his head tight as the boy let out a muffled scream.

Butch made a gagging sound, and Mike looked up just in time to see him vomit onto the bed and slip to his knees as his legs gave out.

"Jesus Christ, Butch," Jesse shouted.

Steve stepped back from the bed and yelled, "Get him out of here."

Mike put the towel and whiskey on the nightstand. JP and Jesse maintained firm grips on the thrashing patient trying their best to stabilize him. Mike rounded the bed and helped Butch to his feet. The stench and mess of the vomit made Mike gag himself.

"Get him out of here. Stat," Steve ordered. "I can't have him passing out in the middle of this."

"Come on, Butch," said Mike finding himself in the absurd position of trying to help this bulky giant to his feet. Butch pushed him aside, wiped his mouth and lurched out of the room.

Tommy alternated between muffled screaming and whimpering. Bubbles of pink foam formed at the corners of his clenched mouth as he huffed and puffed against the washcloth lodged between his teeth.

Still holding the open hemostat in the air, Steve said, "Mike, you're going to have to take that side and hold him down. You'll have to handle the alcohol with one hand when I ask for it."

Mike gripped the boy's arm trying not to see or think about the puddle of gorge on the bed.

Steve dug around in Tommy's back with the hemostat. Sweat poured off him in rivers, and Mike did his best to hold Tommy, dab the doctor's brow and occasionally douse the operation with whiskey. Blood and alcohol flowed on to the towels turning them a sickening reddish brown. Tommy's eyes were wide and wild with pain as he bucked against the three men holding him down. Jesse watched the operation with a stern grimness. JP focused on his younger brother's face, occasionally turning away with tears welling in his own eyes.

Steve mumbled something like, "Got it." then carefully extracted the slug. A fresh flow of dark blood spurted from the wound as if a faucet had been turned on inside the boy. Steve dropped the hemostat and grabbed for the ball of cotton on the nightstand. In his haste, he knocked the ball to the floor.

"Damn it," he cried.

Mike looked with horror at the blood draining from Tommy's back. Steve pressed the drenched towel to the gushing fluid with one hand and bent to retrieve the cotton with the other.

Tommy kicked once violently, then his eyes rolled up. The next moment he lay still, his gaze dully focused on nothing. Steve rose slowly as each man's eyes turned to look at him. The only visible part of his face was just above the mask, but it was enough to reflect a look of intense fear.

A momentary vacuum sucked the air out of the room as each man stood frozen in place. The sudden lull was broken by someone calling from outside.

It was a woman's distant voice calling, "Steve!"

☙   ☙   ☙

After stumbling out of the bedroom, Butch leaned against the hallway wall and tried to compose himself. His stomach churned and his throat burned from retching. He palmed the sweat from his forehead, then wiped the tears from his eyes. He felt ashamed that he had not remained to help with Tommy, but, ironically, he had never had a strong stomach when it came to seeing blood. That is, his own or those few people he cared about.

He had no problem beating someone savagely with his fists or any other weapon. He had made a mess of that guy in Lewistown with a tire iron. Blood had covered everything in the living room when he murdered the family in Livingston. And he had splattered enough faces of his brother cons in fights in Deer Lodge. However, watching the doctor dig into Tommy's back like that was like someone was digging into his own body.

Jesse was bound to be angry with him. Jesse, JP and he loved their little brother. Tommy had stayed out of trouble. The three of them had seen to that. Well, not him so much. Butch had spent much of Tommy's youth in prison. But Jesse, JP and Pop had done their best to steer Tommy in the right direction. The kid looked up to his brothers but had managed to keep on the right side of the law growing up. Butch hadn't really set a very good example, but he had at least made an effort to write to Tommy from prison and encourage him to not end up in jail.

Memories of the days when Tommy was a youngster flooded back in flashes like a slide show. Teaching him tackle football and how to protect himself against bullies by kicking them in the crotch if they messed with him. He recalled the times he'd sit his younger brother on his knee and let him trace the colorful tattoos on his chest and arms, then scare him by roaring when the boy's tiny fingers reached the dragon's mouth. How often had he protected Tommy from his father's drunken beatings? And, unlike his other brothers and so many other cruel bastards, Tommy never once mocked him about his lip or the way he talked.

Now the kid had taken a bullet and was maybe dying in that room. It was their fault. It was Jesse's fault. Jesse had worked out the escape plan. As usual, it was a brilliant Jesse James Toomey scheme. The only problem was that they needed someone on the outside they could trust. Most of the few losers Butch could call friends were neighbors of his in prison. Jesse and JP had some contacts on the outside, but none of them had a full brain between them. So, it came down to getting Tommy to help out. When Tommy told them about his friend who had recently started work for the power company that serviced the prison, Jesse's plan seemed predestined to work.

The brothers went back and forth about involving Tommy. Butch was the main hold out. He'd seen the worst of prison life and didn't want to put their little brother in jeopardy of facing the same existence. In the end, though, Jesse, as usual, convinced them his plan was foolproof and that Tommy and his electrician pal were their best shot at freedom.

The promise of a substantial amount of money and a night of heavy drinking enabled Tommy to talk his friend into assisting him in helping his brothers escape. A contrived power outage, some stolen company coveralls, and the Northwest Energy truck were the boys' ticket out of Deer Lodge. Just like Jesse had planned it.

Tommy's red Mustang was waiting for them on Spring Creek Road. For the first time in fifteen years since he'd been sent to prison, Butch wrapped his arms around his little brother, hugging him so hard he could hear his back bones crack. Choking back tears, Butch climbed in the back with Tommy while JP and Jesse jumped in the front. Tommy's friend in the Northwest Energy truck headed back toward Deer Lodge. With JP at the wheel, the Mustang tore off in the direction of northwest Montana sticking to the back roads winding through the mountains. The plan had come off like clockwork. By now they should have been through Idaho and most of Washington state. But, no; thanks to the incident in Lame Elk, here they were without a vehicle stuck in Bumfuck, Montana, trying to save Tommy's life. Maybe if he'd kept his big damn mouth shut for once and taken it easy on that clerk, they might have gotten out of there without Tommy getting shot. But, as usual, he'd let his anger and bull-headedness rule him.

Why couldn't he be cool and smooth like Jesse? Jesse was the smart one, the handsome one. Even his scar made him attractive to women. Jesse was a natural leader and had friends growing up. He didn't have kids making fun of the way he looked and talked. He didn't see people gaping in shock and disgust when they noticed his torn mouth, or have to suffer the embarrassment of hearing sniggering behind his back at the way his words came out. The giggling stopped once Butch started working out. He had exercised with a vengeance, making the rest of his body as perfect and powerful as possible. No one made fun of him anymore. People knew he had a short fuse, and steered clear of him. It served him well in the prison community. But now that he was out, he needed to control the rage that always boiled just below the surface.

"I'm such an idiot," he bellowed. He pounded his fist against the wall, causing the old plaster to crack. A chunk fell to the floor. It was his fault Tommy got shot, and he wasn't even able to stand there and help hold his little brother. His throat tightened, and he gritted his teeth. *No way am I going to cry,* he thought.

He drew several deep breaths, wiped his mouth and with renewed determination, started back into the bedroom.

Tommy was bucking on the bed, and the three men were holding him down while the doctor dug in his back with some metal instrument. As he worked on the hole, blood burbled out and onto the expanding crimson puddle on the towel. A sharp contraction in Butch's stomach caused his body to convulse, and another acidic bulge moved up his throat. He gagged and turned away, his stomach churning. He charged down the hall and out the back door and launched a spray of vomit onto the deck.

With both hands on the railing, he kept his head low and fought the seething convulsions in his belly by taking deep breaths. *Gotta shake it off. Get hold of myself.* Gradually, the wave of nausea subsided as the curative mountain air washed through his lungs. His body gave a final shudder as he relaxed and took in the panorama of the mountains in the distance.

A late spring strip of snowpack frosted the ridge of the mountain. His gaze drifted down the slope where a few spiky, dark green pine trees stood sentinel-like against the rocky background. Below the tree line, the mountainside was carpeted in a thick covering of firs. Further down and to his right, Butch watched the glistening snake of Thief Creek insinuate itself through the trees. The warm sun and the crisp air cleared his head and restored his strength.

A movement in the timber to his left attracted his attention. At first, he wasn't sure he was seeing what he saw. A hundred yards or so below the inn he could just make out a naked woman soaking in a hot tub surrounded by the trees. Rays of sunlight played off her blond hair, and he saw her graceful back and arms as she rested against the cedar tub, her head thrown back in a restful pose. Steam rose around her in a soft mist. He had been in prison for fifteen years, and other than the ancient hag of a nurse, he had not laid eyes on a real woman except for the occasional two-dimensional sex queen in a contraband porn magazine.

For a brief moment, he considered that he should let Jesse know they were not alone, but the thought was usurped by his own lascivious interest in exploring this vision more closely. Besides, Jesse was busy helping the doctor. It was up to him to check into this new development. Stepping lightly, he moved like a shadow down the stairway to the patio below.

Heather was in heaven. The run with Steve had been glorious. After the stress of the wedding and traveling, the jog through the beautiful scenery had dissipated the negative energy within her as it always did. Following up the exercise in this blissful bubbling tub high in the Rocky Mountains was sweet perfection. She had lost track of time luxuriating in the hot, soothing tub. The bubbling water tickled up her naked body and felt like thousands of tiny fingers teasing her skin. The peaceful beauty of her fragrant surroundings made her feel like she was floating on one of those gigantic white mounds of cloud drifting above her in the azure sky. The only thing missing was her wonderful, anal retentive husband.

Knowing Steve, he had retrieved robes for the two of them and had folded each one perfectly. Now he was probably preparing some gourmet appetizer on the stove. He'd appear any moment with the robes tucked under his arm carrying a tray of warm goodies, a plate of decoratively sliced specialty cheeses and fruits, and an uncorked bottle of fine Pinot Noir that he had allowed to breathe just the right amount of time. Now that she thought of it, she was getting hungry. And more than that, she wanted his company. What was taking him so long?

She leaned her head back, and not willing to open her eyes or turn her face from the delicious shaft of sunlight on her cheeks, she called out for him. "Steve!"

As if on cue, she heard him trying to sneak up through the pine needles behind her. She smiled and kept her eyes closed so she could pretend to be surprised when he arrived.

Butch's hungry eyes devoured every inch of the woman as he drew near her through the trees. A lascivious leer spread across his tattered mouth as he took in her silken blond hair, her skin, her firm naked breasts. Her magnificent breasts. Her arms were spread out along the edge of the tub and her eyes were closed, her head lifted to the sky. The blanket of pine needles had silenced his approach giving him ample time to check her out. He was only a few feet from the tub when he stepped on a small dead tree branch that cracked sharply. A jet black raven scolded from somewhere high above.

The woman turned toward him with a gentle smile, her eyes opening with the dreamy languor of a freshly blooming flower bud. As he expected, though, her smile dissipated and morphed into an all-too-familiar grimace. She recoiled, caught her breath and covered her breasts. Kneeling to her chin in the bubbling water, her wide eyes explored his massive, tattooed torso and misshapen face. He had seen the same look many times in the past. It didn't bother him. Much.

"Sorry if I scared you, miss." His voice was huskier than usual. He struggled with his speech impediment and tried to form a gentler, less threatening smile. He folded his huge arms causing his pectorals and biceps to bulge dramatically, giving the woman a good look at the emerald and scarlet fire-breathing dragon tattoo that snaked around his right arm.

The woman sank even lower so the water covered everything to just below her hazel blue eyes.

"Mind if I get in there with you?" Butch slipped out of his shoes and started to unbuckle his belt.

The blonde moved against the side of the hot tub and lifted her head enough to speak. "Yes, I do mind. Did you see my husband?"

Butch unfastened his pants and dropped them around his ankles. The woman moved further away keeping close to the sides of the tub. "Is Mike your husband?"

"No. My husband is Steve. He just went up to the house to get me a robe. What do you think you're doing?"

"I was going to take a soak with you." Butch grinned, hoping he looked friendly, less threatening. "Your husband's the doctor? He's busy right now."

"Please, I don't have any clothes on. Can you please wait till he brings me a towel and I'll get out? You can have the whole tub to yourself."

Butch hiked up his boxer shorts and started to climb into the tub. "Hey, I don't mind. Don't worry. I ain't gonna hurt you."

Still covering herself, she inched to the opposite side of the tub. He had one leg over the edge when he heard Jesse call from the deck. "Butch, get up here. Now."

"Damn it." He looked up toward the inn then back at the woman, debating his next move. "Gotta go," he said with a sigh. "It was nice meeting you, sweetheart." He climbed out of the tub and hurriedly pulled his pants on, grabbed his shoes and trotted up to the inn.

When he reached the steps, Jesse was leaning on the railing squinting down toward the hot tub."What the hell were you doing?" he asked. "Is there someone down there?"

Butch took the stairs two at a time. "Yeah. Some babe. She's the doc's wife. Very hot."

Jesse's jaw stiffened. "I thought they said there wasn't anyone else here."

Butch shrugged.

Jesse gave a hurried look back down at the woods. "Anyway, get in there. We may have lost Tommy." He pushed Butch into the inn, and they moved quickly down the hall.

~o   ~o   ~o

Butch's heart pounded as he hurried toward the bedroom. *We may have lost Tommy.* Jesse's words echoed in his head, but what exactly did that mean? Surely Tommy really wasn't dead? The anxiety of returning to the scene of the bloody operation was secondary now to the fear of what he might find when he got there.

As he entered the doorway, Butch saw the innkeeper and JP standing on either side of the bed watching the doctor who was alternately pushing on Tommy's chest and bending to breathe into his mouth. A palpable feeling like static electricity filled the room. The knitted brows of both JP and the innkeeper were nothing to the look of desperation and intensity he saw in the doctor's eyes. Sweat streamed down the man's face and dripped on to the still body of his little brother.

Butch turned toward Jesse hoping for some sign of hope. But, Jesse was looking out in the hallway, then closed and locked the door to the bedroom. *Good idea*, thought Butch. Best not to have the doctor's wife see what was going on if she came back in the house.

Jesse and Butch joined the others watching the doctor bend, breathe, then stand back and compress Tommy's chest, counting "1..2..3 . . . " Pushing with both hands. "4..5..6 . . . " Each push made the boy's body bounce on the bed. With each bounce, Butch willed Tommy's eyes to open and for his breath to catch and start up again. His own chest heaved with each compression as if this might be able to help Tommy come to.

His brow knitted in quiet desperation as the exhausted doctor pumped, then shook his head, still counting breathlessly to himself.

"Come on, Tommy," Butch urged, puddles forming in his eyes.

"Don't let him die, Doc," threatened Jesse.

Butch glared at him. Tommy wouldn't be here if it wasn't for Jesse. He would never have been shot. Tommy didn't want to be involved in the breakout in the first place. But Jesse pushed him. He pushed everyone. Now Tommy, sweet Tommy, was paying the price for his brother's pushiness.

The doctor stopped and stood still. He swept his drenched Yankees cap from his head and wiped his brow on his sleeve.

Butch stared at him with bulging red eyes. "What are you doing? Keep pumping."

"Want me to take over, Steve?" Mike asked.

The doctor shook his head. His shoulders sagged. "It's no use." He panted. "I told you he needed a hospital. He lost too much blood and he's died of shock." He sighed deeply and checked his watch. "I'm sorry. I . . . "

Butch's cry filled the room with a frightening keening tone, "Nooo!" He charged over to the doctor, grabbed him by the front of his robe and slapped him so hard a red hand print welled up on his face. "Don't you stop," he screamed. Spit mixed with tears flew from his ragged mouth against the doctor's face. "Keep going. Save him."

He slapped the doctor again. Steve staggered and broke his fall by steadying himself against the nightstand. Butch's own head was pounding painfully in time with his hammering heart. The familiar wave of anger pumped through every nerve in his system. He felt like the Hulk at times like this, sensing his muscles bulging and his body visibly swelling up with rage.

He could tell the doctor felt it. There was that familiar look of dread terror on his face that so many of his past victims had expressed just before he unleashed his wrath on them.

"I'm sorry," whimpered the doctor as he backed up. "Your brother's gone. I did all I could. I tried . . . "

Somewhere behind him he heard JP's voice, "Butch . . . ," as if he were far away in a dream.

He was the Hulk now. The pathetic puny doctor backed away from him, grabbing at the instruments on the towel and sent them clattering to the floor. Steve stepped back once more, then assumed a defensive stance, the shiny scalpel flashing in his hand.

"Stay back." the doc's voice cracked as he held the scalpel in his shaking hand.

"Butch." He heard JP's insistent voice, but there was no stopping him now. *Tommy was dead. We lost Tommy.* His brother was gone and it was the doctor's fault.

With a roar, he charged the doctor, grabbed his wrist with one hand and ripped the scalpel out with the other. His eyes bulged with the blood pumping from his brain.

The doctor screamed, and overwhelmed by Butch's bulk, the two toppled to the floor. As they fell, Butch drove the scalpel into Steve's arm.

The doctor managed a garbled cry for help. Butch stabbed again into the man's chest. Then again. And again. Voices yelled at him from somewhere in the room.

Jesse urged him on, "Do it, Butch! Do it!"

Mike and JP yelled at him to stop.

But his lethal fist kept jabbing savagely and pounding, pounding, pounding. The doctor thrashed beneath him, eyes wide with terror. Then, with a deep gasp, his eyes rolled up inside their sockets and he lay motionless.

Hands pulled at him. The robe lay open on the still body beneath him, and blood dribbled from several neat slashes. Gradually, the painful pulsing in Butch's head subsided and he allowed himself to be pulled off the doctor's body. He fell back on his side, his breath came in wracking gasps. He looked up at JP who held him down. He realized he was sobbing and drooling, but he didn't care. "He's gone," he cried. "We lost Tommy. JP, Tommy's dead."

JP's grip on him softened. "I know, Butch. I know. Relax now. Calm down."

JP rubbed his back. Butch dropped his head into his brother's chest and wept.

Mike was bent over Steve's lacerated body. Without looking up he said, "My God, I think he's dead."

Sniffling, Butch glanced over at his horrible handiwork. The doctor's face and upper body were a mess. The once white robe beneath him was splattered with blood, and a pool was forming on the floor. He looked at his own sticky red hands still grasping the scalpel. He let the knife fall to the floor as a wave of nausea clenched his stomach. His head felt light and he gagged on the bolus in his throat. His stomach muscles contracted again, and he vomited onto JP's pants.

FOURTEEN

O nce she was sure the two men on the deck had disappeared into the inn, Heather climbed out of the hot tub and slipped into her damp running clothes. *What happened to Steve? What was taking him so long?*

She dashed across the yard and took the back stairway up to the second floor, two steps at a time. The door to their room was unlocked. Mike had told them they were the only guests, so they didn't feel compelled to bother with a key. Hopefully, Steve was in the room.

Her heart sank when she saw the room was empty. *He must be downstairs. What did that big muscle head mean when he said Steve was busy? Who was that guy anyway?*

He was in incredible shape for someone his age. She'd seen plenty of studs like him at the health club—in love with their bodies and assuming that every woman lusted after them. They strutted around trying to attract her attention. Flexing their overworked muscles, just like he did. They didn't turn her on, nor did they intimidate her. She could handle herself.

Maybe she had been a little unnerved by him, she admitted, but it was mostly because he'd surprised her. That's all. He was as entitled to use the tub as much as she was. Despite his intimidating image, there was something about the way he spoke to her, like he was embarrassed about the way he talked, and careful at the same time not to make her uncomfortable.

Let it go, she thought. It was too beautiful a day and place to let anything bother her.

She toweled off and pulled on a pair of jeans, a T-shirt and her old Nikes. Her hair was still dripping, so she went into the bathroom and used the fresh towel to dry it.

Her first instinct was to rush downstairs and find her husband. But then she pouted. When those men showed up, he probably forgot about her and got caught up yakking about his precious Yankees with the new guests. Or worse, they were all drinking beer and watching the game on the TV in the Sun Room.

I've got time, she thought. *Might as well look my best for company, and maybe I can make Steve forget about baseball.* She plugged in her hair dryer and reached for the brush. She flipped her head down and let the hot air blow her hair in soft wisps across her face as she brushed.

She hummed as she combed the tangles out. She was proud of herself for choosing Montana for their honeymoon. Such a quiet laid-back environment. It was just what the two of them needed to restore their souls after the exhausting past year of wedding planning and Steve's residency. According to Tuffy, tomorrow was supposed to be warm and sunny and perfect for a ride. Tonight they would have a nice dinner, a bottle of wine, and . . .

Over the noisy whoosh of the hair dryer she thought she heard what sounded like wailing from downstairs. She switched the dryer off and strained to listen. She could hear thumping and yelling coming from the first floor . She opened the door to her room and tiptoed to the top of the stairs. The sounds became more extreme. Somewhere down there a fight was going on. Men were yelling at each other and someone was getting thrashed. She made her way stealthily down the stairs, her hairbrush still in her hand. Her heart hammered in her chest. *Where is Steve?*

Her question was answered by a scream from the first floor bedroom. Her insides turned cold and empty. She had never heard Steve scream, but there was no question that was her husband's voice. She dashed down the remaining stairs. In a panic, she ran down the hall and tried to open the door to the Lewis and Clark Room.

Locked.

She dropped the hairbrush on the floor, gripped the doorknob with both hands and rattled and shook it. Heather pounded on the door and cried out, "Steve! What's going on? Open this door. Open this fucking door."

She stopped and put her ear to the wood. The only sound coming from inside the room was someone crying. She stepped back then charged into the door with her shoulder. She slammed against it sending a wave of pain down her arm, but it didn't budge.

She hammered against the wood and called out again, "Steve! Steve, please open this door."

She heard a metallic click at the lock and watched the knob turn. She stepped back as the door slowly opened, just a crack. The brass chain lock had been slid into place. She strained to look in the room, but her view was blocked by a rough looking man with bright orange hair. A quick gasp escaped her mouth as she took in his battered face, the missing ear and an ugly scar slicing through his pitted skin.

"You need to step off, Miss," the man said. His voice was quiet and firm.

"My husband . . . Let me in there. Who are you?" she demanded, trying to peer around him and into the room.

In the same calm, immovable voice the man said, "Your husband's fine, lady. He's operating on my brother in here, and we can't be disturbed. You can see him when he's done. Now, just go away."

"What do you mean he's operating on your brother? Let me in that room, damn it." Heather could feel the blood rising in her neck, and she glared back at him. She put her fist against the door, ready to push it open.

The man's eyes narrowed, and his jaw clenched. She saw his hand slip to his shirt tail where the butt of a pistol was sticking out. In shock, she stepped back, her eyes darting from the gun to his implacable face.

"Are you sure he's all right? Steve," she called over the man's shoulder. "Are you okay?"

The man's tone, while still firm, lost its calmness. "I told you, he's fine. You can see him when he's done. Now get the hell out of here."

The initial fear she had felt coalesced into a bubbling anger. She felt her body tensing and preparing itself for whatever might come. "Just open this door and let me see Steve," she demanded.

The man glared at her for a moment, then closed the door. She heard the chain lock slide free. Some of her tension relaxed as the door finally began to open.

In a shocking flash, the door swung wide, and she was thrown back by the man in the doorway. His hand circled her throat, and he pushed her against the opposite wall in the hallway, pressing his weight against her. She let out a strangled cry as he crushed her windpipe with his vise-like grip. His hideous face was inches away. His eyes stabbed dangerously into hers, and his voice was menacing. She felt his hot breath and flecks of spit as he snapped at her.

"I told you to get the hell out of here. Now . . . unnnggghh . . . "

His eyes exploded wide as she jammed her knee full force into his groin, actually lifting him up off the floor. She balled her left hand into a fist and swung her arm up in an inside block, knocking his hand from her throat. She immediately twisted her body and jammed his knee with a sidekick. She smiled internally at the intensity of his scream. His reaction to the familiar defensive moves strengthened her self-confidence. When he fell back, she threw a handstrike to the side of his face, knocking him to the floor. He writhed in agony clutching his knee with one hand and cradling his testicles with the other.

Heather stood in a defensive posture over him for only a moment to make sure he was down for the count, then swung around and charged into the bedroom throwing the door wide open. Her body pumped with adrenaline, and her breath came hard. She tried to process the bizarre scene in front of her.

A man lay on the bed covered in blood. She couldn't tell if he was dead or unconscious. Mike was kneeling over something she couldn't see on the floor on the far side of the bed. He looked up at her with concerned eyes and said, "Heather . . . "

The harelip from the hot tub was sitting on the floor slumped against the end of the bed and blubbering. He looked up at her with tears in his eyes and said, "I'm sorry."

Steve was nowhere to be seen.

The only other man in the room charged across from the near side of the bed, grabbed her and pushed her back into the hall. They grappled, and Heather tried to gain a grip on the big man. His muscular arms did their best to control her flailing moves. The two tumbled into the wall, tripping over the other man still cupping his groin, and they both fell to the floor.

"Hold her, JP," the man said through pain and anger-clenched teeth. With some effort, the one called JP grasped Heather's arms and wrestled her to her feet.

She twisted and fought against JP's strong grip, and spat out, "Where's my husband?"

Her answer was a sharp backhand slap from the man whom she had knocked down. He attempted to stand straight, but gingerly favored his knee.

"Bitch," he said and slapped her other cheek. She could feel a trickle of blood run down from where her jawbone had met his blow.

"Jesse. Don't," the harelip called from inside the room.

Heather turned her head and saw the tattooed man in the bedroom rise and approach them, his arm outstretched toward the one called Jesse. She noticed Mike was still kneeling on the floor seemingly immobile from shock. None of this made sense. *Where is Steve?*

"Screw that," said Jesse, still bent over in pain.

Heather turned and, as if in slow motion, saw his arm cocking to punch her in the gut. Instinctively, she tightened her muscles in anticipation. JP had her arms pinned behind her. Jesse jammed his fist into her stomach, but her abs were as tight as a drum. The look of surprise on Jesse's face was gratifying. She plotted her next move.

"Jesse, leave her alone," Butch stepped between them and attempted to hold Jesse off.

Taking advantage of the momentary confusion of the intrusion, Heather kicked out with her foot and connected with Jesse's already crippled knee cap. He howled in agony and collapsed to the floor. In the same instant, Heather smashed her heel on JP's toes, causing him to loosen his grip enough for her to free her arm. Pivoting into him with her hip, she grasped his head and in one deft move managed to flip him up and over her body throwing him against the tattooed man who was bending to help Jesse up.

With the three men tumbled into a pile, she turned and dashed down the hall and out the back door. A loud explosion followed by the door jamb splintering next to her told her that one of the men had retrieved the pistol and was shooting at her. She took the steps down from the deck three at a time and charged into the woods.

Jesse smashed the butt of the pistol against the floor where he was lying. "Son of a bitch. She broke my knee. JP, go get her, damn it."

JP struggled to his feet. "You okay?"

"No, I'm not okay, you idiot. Get that bitch. Don't let her get away.'"

JP scrambled down the hall and out the door.

"What the hell do you think you were doing?" Jesse turned and snarled at Butch, his hand gently probing his knee.

Butch stood up and held out his hand to help his brother up. "I'm sorry, Jesse. But you didn't need to hurt her. The doc was her husband. She was just worried about him. I didn't mean to kill him. It's just . . . I couldn't help myself. I lost control when Tommy . . . " Butch's already puffy eyes welled up with tears. "I didn't mean to kill him."

"He's not dead," Mike said from the bedroom.

FIFTEEN

Heather dashed into the thick timber heading up the mountain. Once she had some cover from the trees, she turned and saw that one of the men had emerged from the inn and was coming after her.

Thoughts tumbled through her head as she ran. *Where is Steve? What happened to him? Who were these thugs?* Her overriding thought, though, was self-preservation. She scrambled up the pine-needled ground. Before she could circle back to find out what was going on with Steve, she needed to rid herself of whoever it was chasing her.

The ground sloped up more steeply the higher she ran. More than once she lost her footing and had to scuttle on all fours over rocks and deadfall. *Keep moving. Moving.*

She couldn't see her pursuer, but she could hear him in the distance as he crashed and cursed his way after her. She was thankful she was in such good shape but running through the underbrush, fear and the altitude were taking their toll. Her breathing came hard, but so did her adrenaline.

She pushed on and eventually found herself on a well-trod game trail winding its way up the mountain. She looked back and caught flashes of the man's orange shirt through the vegetation further down the timber. He was coming on relentlessly, but she had put some distance between the two of them. The game trail would allow her to move more quickly and enable her to find someplace to hide and hopefully lose this guy.

The trail rose steeply and wound up and around a rocky tower of the mountainside. Heather had to slow down and edge her way around the outcropping using one hand to steady herself against the rock wall on the narrow trail. Stones slipped from under her feet and bounced down the slope. How did the wildlife manage to make their way up this precarious path?

Heather looked back to see if she could see her pursuer and tripped over a large rock dislodging it and sending it crashing down the hillside.

"Damn it." Her knee throbbed where she banged it on the ground, and small lines of blood began to form on the palm of her right hand where she had scraped it.

From behind her a voice in the distance called, "Hey. Stop."

A heightened pump of adrenaline replaced the pain in her body, and Heather took off at a run. Rounding the far side of the tower face, she was relieved to see the trail level off into a flatter stretch of high grass and brush. The path ran across a meadow and back into the woods about twenty yards away. In the middle of the field, a pool of crystal clear water sparkled like a turquoise jewel beneath the sunlight. The incongruous thought that she would love to show this to Steve ran through her head. Her heart thumped with the worry of what had happened to him. She pushed on toward the shelter of the timber determined to return to the inn and her husband.

Heather followed the path across the meadow and back into the trees on the other side. The high altitude and her racing heart were exhausting her, and she rested behind a thick lodgepole pine to catch her breath. She bent over with her hands on her knees, panting and trying to think. From off to her left, she became aware of another noise like a small child's whimpering. She held her breath and lifted her head, sharpening her hearing.

A rustling noise came from where she heard the whimpers. The sounds emanated from a few feet away where she had entered the trees. Scanning the foliage, she noticed a bush shaking. At its base lay a large dead tree trunk that was rocking gently back and forth. On the other side of the tree, she spotted a dark brown lump.

It was the lump that was making whimpering and snuffling sounds. She narrowed her gaze on the spot, trying to make out what she was seeing and hearing. The whimpering stopped, and whatever was making the noise stood up.

Two rounded ears and tiny brown eyes turned toward her as the chubby animal rose on its hind legs and sniffed the air. Heather caught her breath and couldn't help smiling as she took in the sight of the cute brown bear cub standing at the edge of the clearing. He stood on his hind legs, his front paws in front of him bent at the wrists as if he was about to play a piano. The cub was just a few feet tall. He lifted his nose and sniffed the air. When he caught sight of Heather, he gazed back at her without moving.

The two stared at each other in silence. Her heart raced, not in fear, but in excitement at seeing this wild animal so close and so cute.

Below and behind her rocks tumbled down the mountainside as the man chasing her neared the bend in the trail. The cub also picked up on the sound and turned his dirt-covered snout in that direction. He sniffed in the air in the direction of the noise. Another sound, nearer and behind the cub, drew Heather's attention. Just inside the dark cover of the trees, a few feet from the cub, she discerned a shadowy movement coming toward the baby bear. Her body froze.

A large black bear, followed by another fuzzy cub, emerged from where she had been foraging and keeping an eye on her baby. She held her nose high, snuffling the soft breeze and headed resolutely toward the cub. When she picked up Heather's scent, she stopped so suddenly her other cub bumped into her rump. Whereas the young bear was non-threatening, this large mother bear emanated intimidating waves of danger as her eyes held fast on Heather. The sow grunted and slapped the ground. The second cub, now alert that there might be trouble, took a step back behind its mother and stared at Heather.

The mother bear moved into position between her and the cubs, keeping her gaze fixed on Heather.

"Go," said Heather, keeping her voice low but firm. She tried to avoid sounding as shaky as she felt.

The bears only stared back at her. She had never seen a bear this close before. The only ones she had ever seen were on a school trip to the Columbus Zoo where they were safely behind an enclosure. Covered with dust, hay and peanut shells, the zoo bears shuffled morosely back and forth behind their bars, snuffling at the snacks people weren't supposed to be throwing at them.

However, up close, she found this mother bear to be extraordinarily beautiful. Her thick black fur glistened in the shafts of sunlight highlighting her through the trees. Her body was massive and all muscle. Her eyes were brown and almost gentle, expressing wariness and warning at the same time.

One part of Heather held her in place in fascination, while at the same time, her heart raced at the obvious danger she was in. Heather felt dizzy with fear and confusion. She tried to recall what the innkeeper had told her to do. Was she supposed to play dead? Make a noise and try to scare the bears off? The only thing she knew for sure was that she shouldn't run, though every fiber in her body screamed at her to turn and get away as fast as possible.

"Shoo. Get away," Heather said with a bit more force and volume. She wanted to wave the animals off but was afraid the movement might incite them to attack.

The mother bear responded with a deep huff. The hair on Heather's neck stood up, and she suddenly felt like she had to pee. She wanted to cry. "Please, just go," she pleaded. At this, the mother bear began to bounce and slap her front paw hard on the ground. Heather slowly backed up from behind the pine tree. Good idea or not, the urge to run was overwhelming her.

"Hey! Stop," a loud voice commanded her.

Heather twisted her head and saw the man who was chasing her emerge from the timber on the other side of the meadow. It was the one called JP. He leaned against a tree trying to catch his breath. The three bears also turned toward the sound. Heather shifted her gaze to the bears and saw that they were fixed on the man who was now lumbering toward them across the meadow.

"Lady, stop. I'm not going to hurt you," JP called out as he ran, apparently oblivious to the fact that there were three bears watching him charge toward them.

The mother bear chuffed more aggressively and repositioned herself between her brood and the running man. With their attention focused on him, Heather decided this was her chance, and keeping her eyes on them, slowly backed away from the bears, gradually moving further down the trail.

JP remained focused on her, and seeing her movement, picked up his speed. Stepping slowly backward, keeping an eye on both the bears and the man, Heather saw him suddenly stand stock still. Despite the danger she felt, Heather stopped and watched the unfolding drama. The mother bear had moved out from the cover of the trees and pounded angrily on the ground. Too late, JP became aware of the bears. He stopped only a few feet away from the trio and started to back up. The sow stomped twice on the ground and began a deep-throated rhythmic humming grunt.

"Look out," Heather found herself calling, despite the threat of JP. Not knowing what else to say she warned, "Don't run."

With a brief glance across at Heather, JP turned on his heels and took off in the direction he had come. With a roar and her cubs following close behind, the mother bear broke from the timber and loped after the man. Throwing a look over his shoulder, JP screamed and dashed across the meadow. In response, the bears picked up their speed, the mother outdistancing her babies. Heather was torn. She knew this was her opportunity to make a break for it, but the fascination and horror of what was transpiring in the meadow held her fast. She felt she must do something, but her head told her there was nothing to do but protect herself.

The mother bear moved more quickly than the man, and rapidly closed the distance between them. While a perverse side of her wanted to see what was going to happen, Heather's brain and thumping heart told her she needed to move. Now. She turned and jogged down the game trail putting distance between herself and the bears. She had only gone a few feet when she heard a series of terrifying screams coming from behind her. The thought of what was happening sent a flush of ice water through her body. She ran like she had never run before, trying as much to escape the bears as the horrific sounds of a human being ripped apart.

Sixteen

ike glared at Jesse who still held the pistol in his hand staring down at Steve's body. "Why don't you put that gun down and help me with this man?" he said.

"He's not dead?" Butch asked, a note of hope in his voice.

Mike glanced at Butch standing slump-shouldered in the doorway. For someone who had wreaked this havoc on the young doctor, Butch appeared surprisingly contrite and concerned. "No, he's not dead. I guess he went into shock and passed out. But we do need to stop the bleeding and get him taken care of. Give me a hand, and we'll take him into the next room."

Jesse remained standing, slightly bent and favoring his damaged leg."Butch," he directed his brother with a nod toward Mike and Steve. He limped to where Tommy lay and sat next to him on the bed, head bowed.

Butch crossed to the side of the bed taking up position at Steve's feet. Mike waited until he was ready, then slipped his arms under Steve's back. The two men lifted and carried him out and down the hall to the next room.

"I'm sorry, man," Butch said, as much to Steve's unconscious form as to Mike. "I just lost it. I didn't mean to take it out on the doc. I know it wasn't his fault. But Tommy's my little brother. He was the best of us all. He didn't deserve to die. He's only a kid. I just lost it," he repeated shaking his head. "I'm such an idiot."

Mike was inclined to agree with him, but he sensed a sincere regret in the man. Besides, this was neither the moment nor the place to fix blame.

"Let's just get him on the bed and patch him up," he said. He opened the door to the Bridger Room. It was a large room with two queen size beds. They laid Steve on the down quilt of one of the beds.

"Fortunately, the scalpel blade is small, so the cuts aren't too deep," said Mike. "Grab the first aid kit from the other room and bring it in here."

Butch nodded and left the room. Mike dampened a washcloth from the bathroom and cleaned up Steve's wounds. They weren't as bad as he had at first thought. As he wiped at the cuts, Steve moaned. Mike glanced at his face and saw his eyes flutter open. He looked confused at first—his gaze explored the room checking out his surroundings. He struggled to sit up, but Mike held him down.

"Take it easy, Steve," Mike said. "We're going to patch you up. Got any advice, Doctor?" He gave a weak smile.

Steve looked down at his wounds and winced. "What happened? Where is that big idiot?"

"Shhh," cautioned Mike, glancing at the door. "You passed out, and we brought you in here. Butch is getting the first aid kit. For what it's worth, he apologized for what he did to you."

"Apologized?" Steve said incredulously. "He almost killed me."

"Yeah, I know, but . . . "

"Who are those guys?"

"I don't know," Mike said, "I think they may be escaped convicts. It's best if we . . . "

Butch lumbered into the room carrying the big kit. The two men looked up at him, and he stopped short at the door.

"Doc," he said. "You're awake." A brief look of relief softened his eyes. "Hey, I'm sorry about what I did. I guess I lost it when Tommy . . . "

"Yeah, okay," Steve cut him short. He turned to Mike and said, "You've got to close these cuts."

"Do you need stitches?"

Steve examined his chest. "Maybe on this one." He pointed at a longer gash that Mike had been holding the washcloth against. I think we can close the rest with some butterfly bandages. Got any in your kit?"

Butch laid the case on the bed and opened it. Mike rummaged through the various sections and brought out a handful of individually wrapped bandages and held them up. "Will these do?"

Steve grimaced in pain and eyeballed the bandages. "Yeah, they should work. There's a suture needle and thread in the other room. You'll need that."

"I'll get it," said Butch and he headed toward the door.

"Bring the bottle of whiskey, the syringe and that little bottle on the nightstand too," Steve called after him.

Butch nodded and hurried down the hallway.

Steve checked the doorway, then whispered to Mike. "Where's Heather? Does she know . . . "

Mike also glanced at the door. "I don't know. She . . . " He hesitated.

"What?" Steve clutched at Mike's arm.

Mike sighed, "I don't know what she saw. All I know is she kicked the crap out of Jesse and took off running out the door."

Steve tried to raise himself up, but Mike held him down. "She did what? What the hell did they do to her? Is she okay?"

Mike laid a calming hand on Steve's shoulder. "Relax, man. There was a struggle, but I don't think she was hurt. She did a number on Jesse and JP and then she ran." Mike thought it best not to mention the gun shot. "JP went after her, but she had a good head start. I don't think if she doesn't want to get caught that he's got a chance. And from what I saw her do to him and Jesse, if he does catch up to her, he's the one who's going to be sorry."

Steve dropped his head on the pillow, rolled his eyes back and stared at the ceiling."Heather . . . "

Mike's thoughts turned to his own wife. Annie would be home in a couple of hours. *What might these thugs do to her?* The idea that they might hurt her caused his stomach to churn. He had to do something. Hopefully, Heather had managed to get away safely, but he couldn't count on that. The safety of his wife and his guests rested with him.

But how was he going to defend them all from these tough bastards? He wasn't a fighter, and even if he was, he'd be no match for the three of them. The phrase *divide and conquer* entered his mind. He needed to deal with each one of these men individually. Break them up. But how?

Butch re-entered the room followed by Jesse who was still limping. They carried the items Steve had requested and laid them on the nightstand. Mike noticed that the gun was tucked into Jesse's pants.

Steve glared at the men as they came near the bed. "What did you bastards do to my wife?"

Butch glanced at his brother and then down at his shoes.

"Your wife is one tough bitch, Doc," said Jesse. "But then, so is my brother here." He nodded at Butch. "My brother, JP, is going to bring her back here. When he does, I'm going to turn her over to Butchie and let him deal with her attitude. He's very effective if you know what I mean."

Steve glared at Jesse, then at Butch who refused to look up. "If you so much as touch her, I'll kill you."

Jesse laughed and said, "Sure, Doc. You do that." He turned to Mike and said, "Whatever you're going to do here, get it done."

The two brothers stepped back as Mike came around to that side of the bed.

"You're going to have to walk me through this, Steve," Mike said.

Steve tried to sit up and winced, then fell back on the bed. "Okay," he said. "First, go wash your hands really well."

Mike hurried to the bathroom and turned the water as hot as he could stand, and scrubbed his hands thoroughly. He dried them and returned to the bedside.

"Do you know how to sew?" Steve glanced up at him with one eye.

Mike gulped and nodded.

"Good. First, clean the wound with the whiskey and dry it with that towel. Then you're going to sew it up with that needle there. It's a little different than a regular sewing needle. It's curved, but it works the same. Stitch me up, then we can take care of the other cuts."

Butch coughed, cleared his throat and said, "I think I'll go outside."

Jesse nodded at him and said, "Yeah, while you're out there see if you can find JP and that bitch."

Steve's eyes looked startled, and he glanced up at Mike. The innkeeper shook his head, cautioning him with his eyes to relax.

"Leave her the hell alone," Steve croaked, trying to sound threatening, though too weak to make it convincing.

Jesse turned back to Steve and said, "Or what? What are you going to do? Oh, don't you worry, Doc. I'm definitely not going to leave her alone. You can count on it. She's tough. I'll give her that. But I'm not letting anyone whale on me like that. Nobody."

Steve tried to rise up on the bed, but his strength had left him. He looked up with pleading eyes at Mike who was nervously threading the suturing needle.

In the distance, a throbbing *chocka, chocka, chocka* could be heard approaching. All three men grew silent, straining to hear. It was the unmistakable sound of a helicopter making its way up from the valley. A glimmer of hope rose in Mike's chest. He glanced at Jesse who limped to the window.

"Listen," Mike said. "That's most likely the sheriff searching for you and your brothers. You need to get out of here. Right? The sooner, the better. I have an idea, but first, you need to call off your brothers and forget about the woman."

Jesse peered briefly at the helicopter then back at Mike. "What's your idea?"

SEVENTEEN

A blood-curdling scream rolled down the mountain from somewhere above, then ceased. *JP?* Butch picked up his pace through the dense underbrush. The woods were thick and the slope steep. Thorny bushes snagged his pants in the overgrown areas, and where no vegetation troubled him, loose rocks slipped under his boots sliding him perilously close to the edge of the narrow trail. His legs ached, and his lungs felt like tiny, ineffective balloons. His lumbering trot slowed to a stumbling walk. He had to pause every few yards and wheeze more of the thin air into his chest. Pine branches whipped his face and naked torso and sweat stung his eyes. Another strangled cry echoed down. Then, silence. He stopped to try to get his bearings and catch his breath. Rather than follow the game trail, Butch decided to shortcut straight up to the top. Snatching at brush and branches, he worked his way up the steep slope. He grabbed a gnarled bush, and its dried branches snapped in his hand. When he gripped it tighter, he felt the sickening feeling of it ripping from the soil. He tumbled backwards and grabbed a low pine branch to catch himself. The branch bent with his weight and snapped. He tumbled down the hillside, clutching at loose dirt and anything else to slow his roll. He grunted and cried out. Rocks, sharp and smooth, sliced and bruised his chest, arms and face as he crashed his way down the mountainside.

With a thump, he slammed into a thick pine tree. He lay still for a moment trying to catch his breath and assess the damage to his torn body.

Using the tree to struggle to his feet, Butch stood and gulped the air. Pine pitch, dirt and blood covered his hands, and his chest heaved with the exertion of trying to breathe in the high altitude. He peered up the slope. The climb back to where he had slipped looked daunting, and he winced as he felt the pain in his bruised ribs with each wheezing breath. He needed a minute to get the strength and motivation to restart his pursuit.

What am I doing, he thought. *I'm fifty-two years old and chasing a twenty-five year old girl through the freaking mountains. For what? For Jesse. Once again I'm taking orders from him and ending up in trouble. Story of my life. We don't need to hurt that broad. We should just let her go. But no, Jesse's got JP chasing her and me chasing the two of them while he stays back at the inn. Typical. How am I going to find JP out here? This whole thing is messed up.*

Ever since he was young, even though he was the oldest, Butch and JP had deferred to Jesse, carrying out his instructions whether it was to steal candy bars from Wilcox' Drug Store or later to rob houses and hold up convenience stores. It was Jesse who egged him on to build his body, to get strong so he could beat up on the kids that Jesse would taunt into fights. Later, Butch was the one that did the rough stuff on the jobs that Jesse planned. He hadn't minded. He actually felt good carrying out those murders, those rapes. Jesse was proud of him. Needed him. All the shame and embarrassment he suffered as a child he channeled into working out, every day, hour after hour. He couldn't be the best looking guy in the world, but he could sure become the strongest. The toughest. He was probably even tougher than Pop. That mean old bastard. He wished the old man were alive today and tried to beat him with that belt. That would be a short battle. Especially toward the end when Pop's smoking, drinking and plain rotten meanness took its toll. He'd become a shell of his former self. A dried up, heartless and lonely shell.

He cringed as a stab of pain jabbed his rib.

After Pop died, Jesse took over. It was like he had inherited the old man's meanness and cruelty. By then, Butch was too big to push around, but Jesse managed to get him to do his bidding. Like Pop, Jesse made fun of the way he talked and looked, but supposedly in fun. Butch knew his brother needed him, and that's what mattered. So, he put up with the teasing and taunting. He'd spent most of his life in prison because of the things his brother made him do.

But now? He was still strong, still tougher than guys half his age, but he wasn't the man he'd once been. He got tired more quickly. His body ached when he got up every morning. He'd usually avoided looking directly in the mirror at his torn face, but now when he did, there were creases and wrinkles and bags under his eyes that were as off-putting as the damnable crevice of his cleft lip. Here he was, battered and out of breath chasing an innocent woman who was only trying to find her husband. The husband that he, Butch, had nearly killed. Once again, his anger had gotten the best of him. And Jesse had taken advantage of that anger, pushing him to do it. Do it. It wasn't the doctor's fault Tommy was dead. It was Jesse's fault. He should never have gotten Tommy involved in the escape. It should be one of them, not Tommy who died.

A squirrel chuckled at him from a branch above his head.

He regretted even having escaped now. Maybe he belonged in prison. He had been respected back in the joint. Nobody messed with him. Nobody made fun of his speech impediment or his face. He was feared. He knew where he stood. He was used to the rhythm and the routine. Even if he and his brothers managed to escape from the situation they were in now, what was life going to be like on the outside? He was getting too old and tired to keep doing the kinds of jobs he used to do. He was fed up with taking bullshit from his brother. At least at Deer Lodge, he was his own man and Jesse couldn't tell him what to do.

He'd had a bad feeling about the escape when Jesse had first brought the idea up. Now, if they got caught, he'd be back in prison, but not in his old position as one of the top dogs. He'd be put in solitary with only thoughts of his wasted life and memories of Tommy to keep him company. And if he didn't get captured, he'd always be on the run.

He was tired. Tired of the running. Tired of Jesse. Tired of being the tough guy. Tired of scaring people.

Damn it! He pounded his fist against the trunk of the tree.

Chocka, chocka, chocka, chocka.

Butch shaded his eyes and squinted at the sky through the tree branches. A helicopter crept its way slowly overhead. A gold insignia and the huge word, "Sheriff" were emblazoned across the fuselage. *They're looking for us.* He pressed himself against the lodgepole pine. His heart hammered against the bark of the tree as the helicopter slowed, hovered briefly and then banked to the left. He watched it make a tight circle.

Sweat streaked down his dirt-covered face. Had they seen him?

The Fears took hold of his guts and twisted like they used to when he was a boy and he heard his father's faltering footsteps coming up the stairs. The old man would be drunk and wanting to take out his anger, disappointment and self-loathing on his son with the screwed-up face. The Fears would come over him, and he knew there was no escaping the slapping and the belt lashings. And worse than the beatings was his father yelling at him, "You make me sick, you freak." *Freak.* Deep inside him the frightened little boy he'd once been wanted to run away and hide. From his father. From the world.

He heard the chopper slowing and descending just up the mountain from him. They were coming for him just like his father used to. His thoughts flashed back to his brother. *Damn it. Jesse, what should I do?*

Eighteen

From his seat in the helicopter, Sergeant Colton Anderson squinted in horror at the scene on the ground below. "Jesus, Harry," he yelled to the pilot. "Take it down over there."

The pilot glanced in the direction where Anderson pointed and peered at the meadow below for a landing spot. He eased the cyclic left and banked lower over the clearing.

The black bear glanced up at the descending helicopter and loped into the woods with her two cubs bounding after her.

"My God. That's a man," the pilot said.

The sergeant nodded back and flipped the switch on the transmitter. "Sheriff. This is Colton. Come in."

The radio crackled back, "Yeah, Colton. This is Sheriff Tate. What's your 20? Go."

"We're just north of Thief Creek, near Saddle Peak."

"Seen anything? Over."

"No sign of the car yet. But we're dropping down into a field here. Looks like someone's been attacked by a bear. Going to check it out. 10-4?"

There was a brief pause from the other end. Then, "Hell, Colton. Is he alive? Over."

Anderson bit his lip and shook his head. He knew the crusty old sheriff wasn't happy about the distraction. He wanted that car found, and he would consider rescuing some hapless unprepared camper a waste of valuable time and resource. He rolled his eyes at the pilot.

"Can't tell. Looks pretty messed up. I'll let you know. Over."

By the time the pilot nestled the chopper into the field, the sergeant had his helmet off and jumped into the tall grass waving in the rotor wash. He kept his head low and made his way to the mangled pile of bloody clothing. He'd seen victims of bear attacks before and wasn't looking forward to what he was about to witness.

As he approached, the victim's arm raised a few inches off the ground then dropped back. Anderson hurried to his side. It was worse than he thought. He couldn't believe the man was alive. Except for a small patch of orange hair, his scalp and face had been gnawed off. His jawbone and teeth were exposed, and one eyeball dangled from its socket. Anderson felt his stomach turn, and he gagged as the man's jaw moved and a groan followed by a wet gurgle drained from his ravaged face. The bears had chewed his arms and legs, leaving them in tatters. His clothes were drenched in blood.

Although as he spoke the words, he knew it was hopeless. "Hang in there, sir. We'll get you out of here." He gagged again as the man's one good eye rolled up and stared at him from the raw meat of his face.

Anderson dashed back to the helicopter and unlashed a stretcher from one of its skids.

"Is he dead?" the pilot yelled over the idling rotors, unbuckling his seatbelt.

"Might as well be. We've got to get him back to Lame Elk. Give me a hand."

"The sheriff's not going to be happy about this."

"We can't leave the guy here," Anderson yelled back over his shoulder. "Sheriff's just going to have to deal with it."

The sergeant had the stretcher open and on the ground next to the victim when the pilot came up. "Damn," he said. "You sure he's alive?"

Anderson shrugged. The two men loaded JP onto the stretcher and carried him back to the helicopter.

Nineteen

From the cover of the trees Butch watched the two officers load JP's body onto the helicopter and lift off. The huge rotors whooshed a tsunami of dust, twigs and dead grass toward him as it revved and rose into the sky.

He dropped back against a fir tree, and a wave of emptiness flushed through him. *JP. Dead.* Now he'd lost another brother. Suddenly, all that remained of the Toomey family were he and Jesse. His eyes burned and itched and he rubbed them with the butt of his hand. Must be the dirt from the chopper. But the tears that welled up and ran down his cheeks were not from the rotors' backwash. He slid to the ground, dropped his head in his arms and began to cry. Such a foreign and yet, distantly familiar feeling.

He hadn't cried since he was a young boy when the kids on the playground danced in a circle around him, mocking the way he talked and his damned harelip. He hated them. He hated his face. He hated the stupid way he sounded. He hated his drunken no-good parents. He hated the world. He hated God.

Then, as now, he had buried his head in his arms and tried to hold the tears back, but they would not be denied. The sniffling turned to blubbering, and then, the long-suppressed anguish and loneliness of who he was turned into a keening wail. A sound so filled with despair and agony the children stopped their derisive dance and slowly dissolved away, leaving him in a small, sad bundle on the ground.

Now, that same flood of long-stifled misery overflowed the dam he had built within him to hold the feelings back, and he wept. He sobbed.

He screamed. He swore. He pounded his fist on the ground beneath him and railed at Jesse for what he'd wrought. For Tommy's death. For JP. For the wasted years he'd spent locked up. For the people he'd hurt. For the people he had killed. For the worthless, soulless life he'd led. His body shook with the wracking weeping of a deeply tortured man. The tears tore at him like pelting acid rain, and he let them come. Let them wash over him. Let them purge the pain and desolation that he had internalized all his life.

With his elbows against his knees, Butch folded his hands together and beat them rhythmically against his forehead as his sobbing reduced to sniffles. Slowly, he lifted his head resting his chin against his hands. His drained body shivered out a last tear.

He sniffed and heard himself whisper, "Help me."

ℒ   ℒ   ℒ

Heather shaded her eyes and looked up through the canopy of trees at the helicopter as it climbed into the bright sunlight. The bold red letters on its fuselage read "SHERIFF." She jumped up and down waving her arms crazily at the rising copter. Although she knew it was unlikely she could be seen or heard from where she stood, she yelled at the top of her lungs."Hey! Help! Hey."

The tail of the helicopter became smaller and faded along with the sounds of its rotors until it was just a glint in the sky. Heather's shoulders drooped, but she continued to watch the chopper disappear from view, trying to will it back.

Damn it. She ran her hands through her hair in frustration and tried to think. It was up to her. She shrugged, sighed and turned back in the direction she had been heading. Back toward the game trail and the inn. Back to Steve.

She reckoned that the trail was not far above her and sloping down. Continuing in the direction she was headed should bring her to the path before long. Without the well-trod game trail to walk on, the crumbly mountainside was difficult to maneuver. Sliding rocks and deadfall slowed her and demanded constant attention. She kept her eyes focused on the ground and her senses sharp.

The woods were alive with sounds. Squirrels chattered at her from the trees and various birds—crows, hawks and some she couldn't identify—cawed, cried and chirped to each other as she moved silently across the terrain. The warm waves of breeze blew the treetops back and forth in a whisper of white noise.

Heather thought she heard a branch crack and stopped in her tracks. The hair on her neck bristled, and her heart thumped faster. She turned her head in one direction then another—back and forward and up the steep slope. Nothing.

She glanced around once more, and seeing nothing, she chalked up the sound to normal woods noises and her physical reaction to overly-cautious paranoia. Nonetheless, an uneasy wariness remained. She headed forward and picked up her pace, keeping her attention less focused on the ground beneath her and more on the surroundings above her.

Suddenly, a rock tumbled from above and bounced across the trail in front of her, and rolled down the mountain. Heather halted and crouched—all senses acute and on guard. She remained motionless except for her eyes which scanned the area above her. She held her breath and tuned her ears to pick up the sounds around her. But, there were no sounds now other than the soft susurration of the breeze far above. No squirrels. No birds. The creatures of the woods seemed to be holding their breath along with her. Vigilant. Expectant.

Heather, still in a semi-crouch, took a few steps then stopped again. Dead-still. Listening. Scanning.

Something.

Something was near. Watching her. Stalking her.

Her arms tingled with goosebumps. A chill shivered down her spine. She remained still as a deer who has picked up the scent of a predator. Not moving. Not breathing. Eyes wide.

A noise above her shattered the silence and made her jerk upright. An electric bolt of fear shot from her feet to the top of her head.

A crow's raucous caw-caw barked down at her from where it perched on a branch. She peered up at the big bird, its head cocked, spying on her with its malevolent obsidian eyes. The bird's cry echoed through the silent woods and traveled up the mountain. Heather's heart leapt as the bird's shroud-like black wings beat the air above her, and lifted it in flight.

The breath she had held so long escaped in a rush. She closed her eyes and held her hand to her chest, which was pounding like a stuttering jackhammer stabbing through asphalt. She took a moment to catch her breath and let her pulse return to normal. She allowed herself a chuckle at her jumpiness. *Just a bird.* Heather straightened her shoulders, looked around to regain her bearings, then set off for the inn once again.

She had not gone far when she found herself back on the trampled surface of the game trail. At last. No more scrabbling over rocks and limbs. It would be easy to jog the rest of the way. She bent to re-tie her running shoes which had loosened over the rough terrain.

Suddenly, two massive arms enwrapped her body and snapped her into a standing position, pinning her. She felt the damp hot skin of a man's chest against her back and his head hard up against the side of her face. The bristles of his whiskers scratched her cheek, and the salty tang of his body odor filled her nostrils

She tried to twist and struggle against him with familiar moves designed to counter such holds, but his vise-like strength allowed her no movement at all. With each gasp of air she took, his grip tightened more, squeezing her to him like some enormous boa constrictor.

"Relax," he whispered throatily, inches from her ear.

Heather gritted her teeth and tried to jerk free. This only caused her captor to clench her even more tightly.

"Stop it. Settle down, lady." The man's speech was strange like he was speaking from high up within his nose. It was the voice of the man at the hot tub.

Heather attempted to lift her shoulders to loosen his bear hug and carry through on a series of defensive moves, but his arms were too low down and too tightly clasped to allow this technique. A head bash was impossible because he had pressed his own skull tightly against hers. The only weapon left to her was her leg. She brought her foot forward and slammed it back into his shin. It was like kicking the side of a skyscraper.

She realized that this man was probably a martial arts expert himself and trying any moves on his muscled body would be like trying to take down a giant oak tree bare-handed.

She squirmed to no avail, feeling her energy sap with each fruitless movement. She was already drained from her hike through the woods, and her reserves were dwindling. Gradually she quit struggling and relaxed.

"That's better," the man said. It was words with an "s" that seemed to give him the most trouble.

"Go to hell." It wasn't much, but her last weapon was her attitude, and she wasn't about to let him overpower that.

But, he did. With a chuckle that ended in a pig-like snort. "I probably will, sweetheart. Look, I'm not going to hurt you."

"Yeah, right," she snapped and tried once again to twist out of his grip.

He pulled her even tighter with a jerk. "Stop," he said. "I don't want to hurt you, but if I have to, I will. And you don't want that. We're going back to the inn. If I need to, I'll carry you. But, I'd rather you walk on your own two feet. Can you do that?"

Unaccustomed to being powerless, Heather pouted and frowned. She realized there was little she could do at this point to get the upper hand. Better to wait for a more opportune moment. She gritted her teeth and nodded her head.

"Good. Smart choice. Now, I'm going to shift you around, and I suggest you don't try anything cute."

His snuffling speech and warm breath in her ear made her stomach turn.

He shifted her body to his left arm. His strength was amazing. She felt and heard him fumbling with his belt buckle. Whatever he had in mind, she had a sinking sense of dread like someone whose car has skidded on ice and is heading uncontrollably into oncoming traffic.

With a flourish, he whipped the belt from his pants and strapped it around her waist. The difference in their girths left a substantial amount of leather dangling which the man pulled tight, causing a slight pinch in her stomach. At the same time, he released her from his hold.

"There," he said. "Now we can have a nice walk back."

She turned and glared at him, regaining her anger. "Who the hell do you think you are?"

Close up she became aware of just how massive this man was. He stood almost two feet taller than her, and his body was a wall of muscle. His badly cleft lip gave him a sinister look, but at the same time, ironically struck a small chord of sympathy in Heather. No doubt, the body building he had done was the result of overcompensation for his impediment.

"You don't want to know who I am, lady. But, tell me, what's your name."

"None of your . . . Ow!"A tight yank on the leather strap around her waist dug the metal buckle into her side. "Heather," she said between clenched teeth.

"Heather. Nice name. I like that."

She flashed a sarcastic smile at him. "And what's your name? Asshole?"

Butch cocked his head, stuck out his lower lip and gave her a hurt puppy look. "Aw, that's not nice, Heather. My name is Butch. I'll say this about you—you're pretty spunky for a little thing. You messed up my brother bad. I haven't seen anyone do a number on Jesse like that in years."

He chuckled. His eyes reflected true admiration for her skills. "You're pretty good. Unfortunately," he continued, "Jesse ain't too happy about what you did to him. That's why he sent JP and me to bring you back."

"JP? Is he the guy with the orange shirt who was chasing me?"

"Yeah. He's my other brother. Or was." Butch went silent and stared at the ground.

"Oh my God. That was your brother? Do you know what happened to him?"

Butch nodded. "A bear got him. I saw it take off when the helicopter landed. I watched them load his body." He glanced up at Heather, his eyes glassy and troubled.

"I'm sorry," said Heather, her voice softened. She started to reach out a comforting hand to his arm, then pulled it back. "There was nothing I could do."

The two stood in silence for a moment.

Butch cleared his throat. "I lost two brothers in one day."

Heather stared at him with wide eyes. "What do you mean? Two brothers?"

It took a few moments for Butch to speak. "My other brother, Tommy. Your husband tried to save him, but there was nothing he could do."

Heather put her hand to her mouth. Butch's anguish was like a dark blanket enveloping the two of them. "Steve? But . . . What happened?"

The look in Butch's hollow stare told her he wanted to talk, but he shook his head and said, "Doesn't matter. We need to get going."

He gently snapped the end of the belt he was holding as if he were urging a horse to move out. He nodded down the trail and captor and captive walked back toward the inn.

Heather kept up the pace behind Butch's shambling gait. She marveled at the tone of his body, but there was a slump to his shoulders and a mantle of an older man's weariness in his posture. Despite their situation, she felt sorry for Butch's losses. She also wondered about what had happened to Steve.

"You know," she said, "you don't need to have a leash on me. I'm not going to try to run away. I want to get back to my husband."

She felt the tension on the belt loosen slightly.

He turned his head but kept walking. "I don't want to hurt you, but I don't want you trying anything funny either. Okay? So, we'll just leave the belt on for now."

Heather stopped in her tracks, causing Butch to halt and turn. "Is Steve all right?"

Butch's eyes shifted from her to his feet. "Yeah," he mumbled. "He's okay. Now."

Heather's breath and heart clenched at the same time. "Now? What do you mean 'he's okay now?'"

A moment of silence filled the forest as their eyes held each other fast. A squirrel's taunting chatter broke the quiet, and Butch dropped his gaze to the ground once more.

Heather's tone sharpened. "What happened to him? What did you do to Steve?"

Still focused on the ground, Butch said, "He came at me with a knife."

"A knife? Steve wouldn't know what to do with a knife. He's not like that."

"It wasn't a knife. It was a scalpel. When Tommy died, I kind of lost it and we got into it."

"What do you mean you 'got into it?'"

"Your husband and I got into a fight. He grabbed his scalpel, then I grabbed it from him, and he got kind of cut up."

Heather's eyes widened. "Cut up? Is he all right?"

The desperation in her voice made Butch look up again into her eyes. "Yeah. Jesse and that guy, Mike, were taking care of him when I left to find you. Heather, I'm real sorry about Steve. I didn't mean to hurt him. Something just comes over me sometimes. I was mad and upset about losing my little brother. I didn't really mean to hurt your husband. I know it wasn't his fault."

Heather noted his eyes shifted away, and more to himself than her, he added, "It was Jesse's fault."

This time it was Heather who tugged on the belt, snapping Butch out of his thoughts. "Come on," she said. "Let's get back to the inn." She took off at quick trot pulling Butch behind her.

TWENTY

heriff Jack Tate slammed his microphone back into its cradle. "Son of a bitch."

He was almost to the Idaho border with the pedal to the metal. He was pretty sure those boys had turned off the interstate somewhere, and that was going to make finding them a pain in the ass. In retrospect, he should have let the staties cover the highway, and he should have stuck to the back roads. His original plan made sense, though. If the Toomeys wanted the fastest route out of the state, they would have headed to Route 2 West. By the time the troopers could make it, them boys could be in Idaho or Canada.

He'd called the border guards to be on the alert for the Mustang. So, he'd taken the route to Idaho, hoping that Colton Anderson might spot them from the chopper if they were traveling off-highway. His one other deputy was about useless, so he'd had Harlan remain in the office manning the phone. Now he was down an important set of eyes because of a stupid tourist wandering around like bear bait.

As the Welcome to Idaho sign loomed ahead, Tate slowed the patrol car and pulled onto the shoulder of the road. He picked up the microphone and called the office.

"Harlan," he barked. "You copy?"

"10-4, Sheriff." Harlan's sleepy voice drawled from the speaker making Tate grind his teeth.

"I just got a call from Colton. He's picked up some idiot got chewed by a bear and is heading back to town."

"Did you say a bear? Damn. Over."

Tate rolled his eyes and sighed, then clicked his mike on."That's right. A bear. Guy's still alive, but just barely. Call the clinic and have them get the ambulance over to the field and get that guy out of there asap. I want that chopper back up in the air in under five minutes. Got that? Over."

"Yes sir, Sheriff. I'll let them know. Over."

"Five minutes, Harlan. Any word from Highway Patrol or the border? "

"No, sir. 'Fraid not. You have any luck? Over."

Would I be calling you and asking you these questions if I'd had any luck, you moron? "No, Harlan, I haven't had any luck. I'm going to head back. Maybe check some of the side roads. I'll keep you posted. Get on the phone to the clinic. Over and out."

"Yes, sir. Will do. Over and out."

Tate gunned the accelerator, cranked the wheel to the left and bounced across the median heading back the way he'd come. He shook his head. *Harlan. Freaking Barney Fife!* The white cruiser streaked east.

TWENTY-ONE

nnie Preston swept a loose strand of hair behind her ear, leaned on her arms on the Lame Deer Health Clinic reception desk and let out a long sigh.

"You look pooped, Ms. Preston," said Madison in her ever-cheery high school voice.

Annie rolled her eyes and nodded. "This has been a day, Maddy." She glanced at the clock on the wall and said, "I'll be glad when it's over and I can go home."

Madison pouted her lower lip sympathetically. "I guess so. I heard about Mr. Loomis. I can't believe he got shot. I'm glad they brought him in before I started."

Annie saw her blush and catch herself.

"I mean, I'm sorry he got killed and everything, but I wouldn't want to see his dead body. He was nice. I liked him."

"I know," said Annie. "He was nice. He didn't deserve to be shot."

"Did they catch those guys who shot him?"

"I don't know. I haven't heard. After they brought him in, we had a sprained ankle, a dog bite and a rancher who almost cut his thumb off."

Madison wrinkled her nose, "Ewwww."

Annie continued, "Yeah, and that was just this morning. Before you got here, Jimmy Carlson's mom brought him in with some stomach bug, and he threw up in three different places."

Madison wrinkled her freckled nose. "Gross."

"And, of course, Dr. Haroldson is not in today. So, it was pretty much just me holding down the fort. Again."

"Well, at least Mrs. Thorsen was here today. I'm sure she was a big help." Madison glanced at Annie conspiratorially, stifling a giggle.

Annie raised an eyebrow, then burst out laughing, to which Madison responded with a hearty chuckle. "Oh, sure. Emma was a gigantic help. She spent her usual three hours in the ladies room 'reading my stories.' Then spent most of the rest of the time 'puffin' my coffin nails' on cigarette breaks out back or in the bathroom."

Madison covered her mouth and giggled. "You sound just like her. You're funny."

"Well, you need a sense of humor in this place, that's for sure."

"They should hire more help. It's not fair you have to do so much."

"That's the way it is in a town this size, I'm afraid. I'm glad we have you."

Madison smiled back at her.

"I'm going to get a cup of coffee. Want anything?" Annie headed into the file room that doubled as a kitchenette.

"No thanks, Ms. Preston. Oops, there's the phone. Good afternoon. Lame Elk Health Clinic," Madison said brightly.

Annie rinsed a mug and poured what was left in the carafe. There was only half a cup of lukewarm coffee, but she didn't feel like making another pot. She leaned against the counter, resting the back of her head against the cupboard, and sipped the gritty brew.

It certainly had been a trying day. Working at the clinic was exhausting, but the town needed her. With only a part-time doctor to minister to its residents, Lame Elk was lucky to have her. One more hour before she could head back home. A soak in the hot tub and a late dinner with Mike would be heaven. She was glad they only had the young couple as guests. She didn't feel much like socializing.

"Ms. Preston," Madison called from the front.

"Ugh," Annie grunted and dumped the dregs of the coffee into the sink.

Madison had her hand over the phone's mouthpiece. "It's Harlan. He said they're air lifting a guy who's been attacked by bears here, and they need you to have him picked him up at the airfield."

"A bear attack? Good grief. Hand me the phone."

Madison passed the receiver across the counter.

"Harlan? This is Annie Preston. How bad is he?"

"I'm not sure, Ms. Preston. The sheriff just said he'd been chewed up pretty badly."

Annie lifted her eyes to the ceiling and shook her head. She glanced at her watch. Less than an hour until she could finally have gone home. And now this. She let out a deep sigh.

"Well, we don't have the facilities here to handle something like that. He probably will need surgery They should air lift him to the hospital in Whitefish or Kalispell."

"Sheriff said he needs the clinic to pick the fellow up at the airfield and get him out of there in under five minutes. There's no time to go to Kalispell. He needs the chopper to search for those killers."

Annie bit her lip so hard she started bleeding. *Damn Harlan and his slow drawl. Damn Sheriff Tate. Damn Dr. Haroldson. Damn the convicts. Damn this tiny town.*

"You tell the sheriff to fly that man to a proper hospital. Dr. Haroldson is out of town, and I'm the only one here."

"I'm sorry, Ms. Preston, but the sheriff was very specific. He needs that helicopter, and he needs it now. The guy might even be dead by the time the chopper lands, so it won't really matter."

Annie rolled her eyes and stared with disbelief at the phone in her hand. "Harlan . . . "

"I can hear them now, Ms. Preston." Annie could also hear the thrumming sound of the approaching helicopter overhead. "You better get the ambulance over here on the double."

"Harlan . . . " Annie yelled into the phone, but the deputy had already hung up.

Annie ground her teeth so hard her jaw hurt. She banged the phone into its cradle making Madison jump.

Why do these things have to happen when I am the only one on duty? Why did it have to happen now, at the end of the day? She just wanted to get home. Back to the peace and quiet of the inn and Mike's laidback calmness. Most times, his languid style was frustrating, but on days like this, she wanted nothing more than to curl up and lie on the couch in front of the TV with him. Half an hour more and she would have been on her way. Maybe Harlan was right. Maybe the idiot would be dead by the time they got him here.

Madison looked at her with concern."Anything I can do to help, Ms. Preston?"

She realized her fist was clenched so tight her knuckles were white. The nurse in her head scolded her for thinking so selfishly. She sighed deeply, expelling her personal frustration with a long exhale.

"Yes, Maddy. Get someone at the fire station over to the air field to pick up the patient. I'll try to get hold of Dr. Haroldson. Then call my husband and let him know I'm going to be late.

Annie stepped outside and speed-dialed Dr. Haroldson on her cell phone. As she expected, his voice mail message said he was unavailable and instructed the caller to leave a message, and the doctor would reply as soon as possible. In case of emergency, they should call Nurse Annie Preston at the Lame Deer Health Clinic.

"Great," mumbled Annie lifting her eyes skyward and shaking her head.

From up the street, she heard the ambulance wail out of the tiny garage that served as the volunteer fire department and head to the airfield behind the police station.

Returning to the clinic lobby, she saw Madison with a puzzled look on her face hanging up the phone. "What's the matter, Maddy?"

"I don't know. I called your husband, but there was no answer, and the answering machine never came on."

"Terrific. He was having trouble with the phone this morning. It must still be out. I'd better call the phone company. Can you look up their number?"

Annie went into the examining room to make sure their meager supplies were ready for the bear attack victim. Poor bastard.

The clinic door flew open, and two of the men from the fire department rushed in carrying a stretcher bearing a badly mauled man.

Madison dropped the phone book on the desk and leapt up. "Oh my gosh," she said, her hand covering her mouth. "Take him into the examining room."

The men lifted the victim onto the bed. As they did, his partially severed arm tore away from his shoulder and fell to the floor. The younger fireman, Annie couldn't remember his name, was as pale as a sun-bleached cow skull, and his eyes rolled like a spooked stallion. She was afraid he'd faint any moment.

"Thank you, boys. You two can get out of here now," she said.

The boy fairly tripped over his own boots in his rush to leave the room. She could hear him gagging in the lobby. Madison remained standing in the doorway with her hand still over her mouth, gaping at the tattered mess on the bed.

"Maddy," Annie said. "Remember how I showed you to do a tourniquet? Get over here and get a tourniquet on what's left of this man's arm."

Madison whimpered, but dutifully crossed the room and got the tourniquet band from the cabinet.

Annie stepped back to survey the damage and drew in her breath with a gasp. For the first time, she realized that most of the man's face was gone. The bear must have been massive. She could see where its teeth had scraped much of the scalp and face off in one bite. All that was left of his hair was a stringy orange mullet at the back of his head.

It was hard to believe he was alive. She could see he was in hypovolemic shock. He was still breathing, though slowing down rapidly. His eyeball turned toward her in its socket, and his torn jaw moved. At first, she thought he was moaning, but then realized he was attempting to speak. She couldn't make out what he was saying. She bent closer, and through the gurgling in his throat she made out a single word.

It sounded like, "Jesse."

Annie fit her stethoscope into her ears and pressed the chest piece to the man's breast in time to hear his final breath.

TWENTY-TWO

Mike's hands trembled as he sewed up Steve's wound. He winced as he stuck the sharp surgical needle into the man's chest as if he were piercing his own skin. How he wished Annie was here. She'd have no problem at all with the suturing. He wasn't cut out for this. Or for dealing with escaped convicts for that matter.

Mike Preston was a peaceful man. In college, he had marched in protest against the war in Vietnam. He took pride in the fact that he had never been involved in a fist fight. Although he now lived in one of the most desirable places in the country for fishing and hunting, he had never taken up these activities as he was committed to bringing no harm to any living creature.

His father-in-law often tried to cajole him into joining him on his hunting forays, coming close to insulting him with his not-so-subtle jabs at Mike's manhood, bragging about his daughter's early introduction to guns when she was a child.

Steve flinched and cried out as Mike pulled the stitching too tight.

"I'm sorry, Steve."

Be careful. Stay focused. Mike hated this. God, he wished Annie was here to do it. She was the gutsy one.

While proud of his pacifism, Mike sometimes felt secretly doubtful about his courage. Was it courage or cowardice? He had spent his lifetime avoiding conflict. As a boy, he'd run away from the playground bullies. When his college roommates used to get plastered and pick fights with other drunks, Mike would steer them out of harm's way and get them back to the dorm. During faculty meetings at the university his colleagues would get in heated arguments about this policy or that, or tirelessly debate innocuous issues, causing him discomfort, even at the verbal jousting.

There were times that he wished he had the chutzpah of his roommate and other men to stand his ground and get in someone's face, or if necessary, haul off and punch some bully just because. The last time he had felt that strongly was when the dean at his school, that smarmy sycophant, had turned down his petition for tenure in favor of the hot young Chaucer assistant professor he was sleeping with. Even then, when he had all the ammunition he needed to defend his position, he meekly accepted his situation and said nothing. His defiant action was to resign in self-righteous indignation, hurting no one but himself. And Annie.

She tried to talk him into fighting the dean's choice. However, when he showed no desire to plead his case, she had silently accepted his decision and dutifully followed him to the hinterlands of Montana where he would never have to confront another soul. Although they never spoke of the situation, Mike sensed that Annie had lost some respect for him due to his timidity. A trait that he had always worn as a badge of honor now seemed like an albatross around his neck.

"Come on. Hurry it up." Jesse's impatient voice brought him back into focus.

"I'm almost done," Mike said and busied himself in his task while trying to get a handle on his situation and what to do.

He faced the test of his life and his dovish approach. These were violent men. Far worse than the playground bullies. They had nearly killed one of his guests and were hunting down the man's wife intent on harming her for standing up to them. And what had he done to stop them? Nothing.

Soon, his own wife would return home. And what then? Maybe they would simply take the keys to her car and leave her, him and his guests in peace. A glance up at Jesse's evil face told him that this was wishful thinking. The man looking at him for answers was a take-no-prisoners gorilla. It was highly unlikely that Jesse and his brothers would leave the inn without disabling their chances for reporting their whereabouts to the sheriff. At best they would tie them up. At worst . . .

"Well?" said Jesse. "What's your idea?"

Steve jerked as Mike's hand jittered the needle into his skin. Mike winced and swallowed. His half-formed plan tumbled out of his mouth. "I don't think the sheriff can see your car from the helicopter where it is lying under the cover of those trees."

"Yeah. So?"

"Besides, the chopper took off back east, so they may be looking for your Mustang in a different direction. My neighbor is about five miles from here. If you take my four-wheeler you can get to his place and take his car. Then you can come back and pick up your brothers and get away."

Jesse stared out the window and appeared to be giving some thought to this plan.

"And what do I do—leave you here unguarded? I'll wait till my brothers get back."

Mike's stomach tightened. He hadn't expected Jesse to not fall for the bait. "I'm not going anywhere. I've got to stay here and take care of the doctor's wounds. You need to get going. You don't have time to wait for those guys. You've got to hurry."

"I ain't leaving you alone. The doc ain't going anywhere. Throw some bandages on the rest of those cuts and then you're coming with me. JP and Butch can keep an eye on this guy and his wife when they get back. You and I will pay a visit to your neighbor, and you can tell him you need to borrow his car. That way, I won't need to take it by force, if you know what I mean." For emphasis, Jesse wiggled the pistol in Mike's face.

Mike's heart was beating like a tom-tom, and his stomach felt like it was being attacked by a swarm of killer butterflies. He hadn't counted on being taken hostage. He had figured the four-wheeler, already low on gas, would die before Jesse reached the Swanson place, giving him plenty of time to disable the other two brothers before he returned— somehow. He hadn't figured that part out yet. Whatever, he couldn't let any more harm come to Heather, Steve or Annie. But now, his half-formed idea would be dismantled if Jesse took him with him. He had to think of something fast. His mind raced.

"I can't go. There's no place for me to go. I have to stay here and finish this. And I can tell your brothers what the plan is when they get back." Mike's heart was thumping so hard he felt certain that Jesse must be able to hear it.

"I'll leave JP and Butch a note. They'll wait. You're coming with me."

Mike stood in front of Jesse. Even stooped, Jesse was a foot taller than Mike and probably had fifty pounds more on him. Despite the churning in his belly, Mike narrowed his eyes and stuck out his jaw.

"I'm staying here with Steve."

A smirk twisted its way up the right side of Jesse's face. "There's no need to stay with him if he's dead. Right?

Jesse stepped closer to the bed, pointed the gun at Steve's chest and pulled the hammer back. The metallic click set off a trigger in Mike's head and, without thinking, he kicked the gunman in his already wounded knee.

Jesse cried out and crumpled to the floor, dropping his gun as he fell. The pistol skittered across the floor. Mike dove for it. He felt a rush of energy and triumph wash through his body as his hand closed around the solid handle of the weapon. He had never held a pistol in his life and the sense of power it gave him was incredible. His hand shook, not from fear, but from an electric sense of being the one in control. The strongest one. He pointed the gun at Jesse who had stopped writhing on the floor and was now looking at him in abject fear.

"No," Jesse cried with his hand uplifted in protection.

The gun exploded, throwing Mike's hand in the air. With the impact of the shot, his hands and ears tingled numbly, and his surprised brain screamed, *What have I done?*

He looked down at Jesse's body expecting him to be lying motionless in a puddle of blood. But the man reached out and grabbed at him. He had missed! *How could he miss at such close range?*

Before he could ponder this question further, Jesse grabbed his leg and yanked him to the floor. From out of nowhere, Mike felt a sickening thud in his belly and the air disappear from his lungs.

Jesse's arm slipped around his neck and pulled him tight against his body. His other hand reached out and grabbed the pistol from the floor and held the barrel against Mike's head.

"Nice try," Jesse hissed into his ear. "All right, tough guy, we're going to get up, and you're going to drive me to your neighbor's house. You're going to talk him into lending you his car. And you're not going to give me anymore bullshit. Are we clear?" He dug the muzzle into Mike's skull for emphasis.

Mike nodded once. With each labored breath, he felt more empty. Hopeless. Ashamed. In an instant, he'd gone from having the power, the guts, the balls, to being subdued and defenseless. *Idiot! Useless. Weak. Idiot.* He'd blown the chance to carry out his plan. Now he had no choice but to submit. Maybe he'd get another opportunity. Maybe he could come up with another plan. Maybe. But, for now, he had to be the weakling. Again.

The two men got to their feet. Jesse kept the gun trained on Mike.

"You finish patching him up," he indicated Steve with his head, "and I'll write a note for JP and Butch for when they get back. You got some paper and a pen?"

"Over there on the desk."

Jesse shuffled painfully to the desk while Mike finished tending to Steve's cuts. As he put the last bandage on Steve's chest, the doctor looked up at him with gratitude in his eyes.

"Thanks, Mike." He glanced at Jesse across the room scribbling at the desk. In a quieter voice, he whispered, "Thanks for stopping him. He would have shot me. Please don't let them hurt Heather." A tear rolled out of his eye. "Please, man."

Mike put a reassuring hand on his shoulder. "Don't worry. I'll take care of it. It will be all right." He spoke the words, but there was no conviction within his heart. He hoped Steve couldn't sense it.

"All right," Jesse said dropping the pen on the desk. He folded the note and said, "Where can I put this?"

"There's a clip on the door for notes. Put it there."

"You put it there." Jesse thrust the note into Mike's hand, then hobbled to the bed.

As Mike crossed to the door, Jesse began tearing the bed sheet into strips.

"Okay, Doc," Jesse said. "We're going to make sure you get plenty of bed rest until we get back." He proceeded to tie the strips of sheeting around Steve's ankles and wrists and tethered him securely to the bed.

Steve's eyes flashed as the last strip yanked his foot in place. "You leave my wife alone, you asshole."

Jesse grinned back. "Oh, Doc, I promise I won't hurt her. Even though she mangled my leg."

Steve's brow furrowed doubtfully.

"No," continued Jesse, "I don't hurt pretty women. I leave that to Butch. He likes to play with them a bit before he finishes them off. He hasn't been able to play with any ladies for years since he's been locked up. I'm sure he'll take good care of her."

Steve twisted against his restraints. "You son of a bitch. If you or your brothers do anything to her, I'll kill you."

"Oooo. You're scaring me." Jesse chuckled then turned toward the door. "Let's go, Mike."

Mike gave Steve a tight-lipped nod, then led the way out with Jesse shuffling behind.

As he let the screen door close, a deafening explosion made Mike jump. He turned and saw Jesse lowering his pistol after firing it into Steve's room.

"My God! You . . . " he said and attempted to go back in the house. Jesse stood in his way and shoved him toward the steps laughing maniacally. The scarred and hideous face and the man's evil outburst of laughter made Mike feel he had met the devil himself.

Jesse gingerly mounted the four-wheeler, and Mike settled in front. He turned the key and pressed the ignition. The ATV rumbled awake.

"Make it fast, tough guy. Or you're next."

Mike set his jaw, twisted the throttle and the four-wheeler churned out of the driveway following two ruts into the timber behind the house.

TWENTY-THREE

With the phone to her ear, Annie tap-tap-tapped the pencil on the counter in the examining room and watched the big red second hand hop its way around the clock face. Finally, Harlan's sloth-like drawl answered. It sounded like he had a mouthful of food. She pictured a half-eaten bear claw pastry in his chubby hand.

"Sheriff's Department. How may I . . . "

"Harlan, this is Annie Preston. Is the sheriff there?

"No, ma'am. He's not."

Annie rolled her eyes and sighed. "Well, do you know where he is? I need to speak with him."

"I believe he's still out looking for those escaped convicts. Unless he stopped for coffee or something. How's that fella from the bear attack doing? Did he make it?"

"No, he didn't make it. That's what I need to talk to the sheriff about." She could tell he'd taken another big chomp of pastry.

"Gee, that's too bad. Pretty messed up, huh?"

"Yes, pretty messed up. Do you have an ID for him?

"For who?"

Annie balled her hand into a fist and stabbed the pencil point into the note pad breaking the tip. She clenched her jaw and said, "For the man from the bear attack. Do you have an ID for him?"

"Oh. No, I sure don't, Ms. Preston. They just flew him in here and rushed him over to the clinic's all I know. Did you look in his wallet? He should have a driver's license or something."

She bit her lip to keep from screaming. She took a breath, then spoke into the phone like she was talking to a six-year-old. "He doesn't have a wallet, Harlan. I would have checked that. He doesn't have anything on him. That's why I'm asking. Where exactly did they find him?"

"Umm . . . " she heard Harlan shuffling through papers on his undoubtedly cluttered, crumb-covered desk. "Here it is. The chopper was doing recon—that's reconnaissance—over toward Elk Peak. They found him in Jacob's Meadow just up from Thief Creek. He was . . . "

Her heart skipped a beat, and her insides felt like an elevator dropping from a broken cable. The deputy kept jabbering, but she wasn't listening. Jacob's Meadow was just north of the inn. There were no other dwellings in that area other than their B and B. It was a pretty spot, but remote and on their private property—not a place that strangers would be wandering in.

Unless they were from the inn.

She lifted the sheet from the mangled face. It definitely wasn't Mike, but what about the new guest? There was too much damage to make out any identifying facial characteristics. The only recognizable feature was the man's distinctive, outdated, red-haired mullet. She felt a moment of relief. It wasn't her guest. Then who?

Her mouth went dry, and her intestines twisted like they were on a turning spit. "Do you have a description of the escaped cons?"

More papers shuffled. "Uhh . . . Four men. Brothers. Thomas Toomey—five-eight, nineteen years old, short red hair, blue eyes; Butch Toomey—six three, fifty-two years old, cleft lip, short red hair, blue eyes, tattoos on arms, torso and back;—Jesse James Toomey—six two, forty-five, blue eyes, scar on left cheek, missing ear, short red hair. Hey, Jesse James—like the outlaw."

Jesse. Wasn't that the name the victim said just before he died? Her breath hitched.

"Looks like they all have red hair and blue eyes. And John Philip, aka, JP Toomey—six foot, forty-one with long red hair and a lady tattoo on his right buttock."

She cradled the receiver in the crook of her neck and tore at the belt on the man's tattered trousers. Madison watched wide-eyed as Annie gripped the waist band and yanked the pants down, exposing the man's backside.

She gasped and covered her mouth with her hand. The phone clattered to the floor as she stepped back. The bear's claws had left a ragged gash in the man's rear end, slashing diagonally across a tattoo of a bare-breasted woman doing a hula in a grass skirt.

Her breath came in short gasps.

Madison raised her eyebrows in concern. "Are you okay, Ms. Preston? What is it?"

She looked at the young girl with eyes wide as if searching for some answer. From the floor, a distant voice called, "Hello? Ms. Preston? Hello?"

She glanced from Madison to the phone, then snatched the receiver from the floor. "It's him," she barked into the phone. "Harlan, it's him."

"Huh?"

"The man with the tattoo. He's the bear victim. He's here."

There was a pause at the other end. "You mean the guy you've got there is one of the Toomey brothers?"

"Yes, you idiot. It's him. The others might be up at the inn or at least nearby there. You need to get hold of the sheriff and tell him."

Harlan's voice sounded hurt. "I'm sorry, Ms. Preston. I didn't understand what you were saying."

Annie took a deep breath and let the air out slowly. "I apologize, Harlan. I didn't mean to call you names. I'm just worried about my husband. I'm truly sorry for what I said. But can you please let the sheriff know that you found one of the escaped convicts up near the Thief Creek Inn and that my husband and our two guests are up there and may be in danger?"

"You betcha. I'll call him right now. You should call your husband too."

It felt like a bowling ball dropped into her stomach with a thud. "I can't."

With a fresh wave of panic, she suddenly realized that the reason the phone was dead might not have been a technical problem after all. "Oh my God," she said. "I have to go."

She hung up the phone and rubbed her forehead. *My purse. My purse. Mike.*

She tried to collect her thoughts and stared at the young girl standing with her eyes wide and confused at the door. "Madison, I've got to leave. I'm sorry. Call Dr. Haroldson on his emergency number and leave a message that he needs to come take care of this body. Lock the door behind me and don't let anyone in except the sheriff or Dr. Haroldson. This is one of the escaped convicts from this morning."

Madison covered her mouth with both hands, and Annie's heart sank at the look of wild-eyed fear in her eyes. "I'm sorry, honey. But I have to go. I'll call you just as soon as I can."

The teenager nodded her head. "Okay. You go. I'll be all right."

Her trembling voice said differently, but Annie couldn't wait any longer. She grabbed her purse, fishing for her car keys and pushed through the clinic exit. The door locked behind her as she ran to her van.

Twenty-four

The four-wheeler bounced along, riding the crests and troughs of the primitive trail like a small boat navigating rough seas. Mike had decided to take this back route rather than the road in order to better his chances of running out of gas and hopefully getting some advantage over Jesse. He would try to take him physically, though the thought seemed ludicrous. Or, more hopefully, perhaps he'd be able to lose the bastard in the woods and make it back to the lodge on his own.

Old trails branched off along the way, some heading higher and some lower. Mike took the rockiest ones that required the slowest movement.

As they lurched sharply from side to side down one particularly steep section, Jesse yelled in his ear, "Why are we going through this crap?"

Mike yelled back, "Short cut. It's the most direct way to the neighbor's place. We'll hit a logging trail soon that will take us to a regular road."

Within minutes, they found themselves on a well-worn logging road, and Mike opened the throttle. They bounced along the trail until it emptied out onto a wide gravel road.

The chubby wheels of the four-wheeler kicked up a cloud of dust behind the two riders. Mike squinted against the hot wind and the occasional sting of a bug whipping across his face as they sped down the gravel road. He had to slow down for the switchbacks but opened the throttle full on the straightaways. The needle on the gas gauge jiggled deeper into the orange warning area. He hadn't expected to make it this far, but there was no way they would make the ten more miles to Caleb Swanson's place. Mike's brain worked feverishly to come up with a strategy for when the motor would finally choke and stall. He had to be prepared.

Too late.

The engine coughed and slowed. Mike cranked the throttle all the way, and the four-wheeler picked up speed again for a few feet, but then sputtered, jerked twice and died.

"What the . . . " Jesse said. "Are you out of gas?"

"I guess so," Mike said.

"Shit. How much further?"

"Probably another ten miles or so."

Jesse climbed off the back and circled the ATV, kicking rocks and cursing as he went. "Don't you have a reserve tank on this thing?" Jesse asked and bent to inspect the four-wheeler's engine.

Mike felt the rising tension in his neck and all the synapses in his body firing like a thousand spark plugs as his mind and body readied him for action. It was now or never.

He swung his boot up into Jesse's face, kicking him off balance. He leapt off the ATV and onto Jesse's body. The two tumbled to the ground.

Mike drew strength from some unknown source and grappled with Jesse, trying to wrest the pistol from his belt. They thrashed in the dirt, grabbing at each other and landing punches when they could. Mike felt all his frustration and anger driving his arms and hands to do their best. However, Jesse's strength and experience at fighting left him outmatched. An elbow jabbed into his solar plexus and knocked the wind out of him. He lost his grip on the other man's shirt. In one swift move, Jesse pulled his gun and stood over Mike, pointing it at him.

Both men's breath came hard. Mike shielded his eyes from the bright sunlight. His heart hammered against his bruised chest.

Jesse glared down at him. "That's twice you've gotten the drop on me. It won't happen again."

Mike's heart pounded, and his body shook. When Jesse pulled back on the hammer of the gun, his bladder let go.

TWENTY-FIVE

As they broke from the timber, Butch let go of the belt round Heather's waist. She was already charging toward the steps to the inn anyway. He loped behind her and climbed the steps one at a time, unlike Heather, who leapt up them two at a time.

"Steve," she called, flinging open the back door.

Butch heard a raspy response from the room down the hall and saw Heather hurry toward it. "Jesse?" he called. There was no reply.

He watched as Heather flung open the door to the room.

"Oh, my God! Steve!" Heather cried.

Butch hurried to the room expecting to see Jesse. Instead, the only person in the room other than Heather was Steve. His hands and feet were bound to the bed. His wife bent over him crying and hugging his head.

Averting his gaze, Butch noticed the note with his name on it clipped to the door. Before reading it, he glanced at the bed and saw Heather untying Steve's bindings. He shrugged and unfolded the note.

Butch and JP—

Have gone with Mike to get a car. We'll split when I get back. Hang on to the bitch till I can take care of her myself. Butch—feel free to do

what you want with her until then. Just let me be the one who finishes her off. You can do her husband anytime.
—JJ

"Screw that," he said and crushed the paper in his fist.

At the sound of his voice, Heather twisted around and hissed at him. "You bastards. How could you do this? He tried to save your brother's life." She angrily worked at the knot on the strip of bed sheet at Steve's foot.

Butch crossed the room and gently moved her out of the way. He gripped the sheet between his hands and with one quick movement, snapped it apart as if it were nothing more than a wet tissue.

"I am sorry, Heather. You're right. He did his best to help Tommy, and what we did . . . what I did . . . wasn't right."

Heather stood back, and Butch went round to the remaining straps, releasing each one as he spoke. "I haven't done anything 'right' since I was a kid. My life has been a series of doing the wrong things. Mostly things Jesse had me do."

"You don't look like someone who could be told what to do by anyone." To Steve she said, "Honey, I'm going to get you some water," and left the room.

Butch smiled and shrugged self-consciously. "You okay, Doc?" he asked.

"I've been better," Steve grumbled as he massaged the red rings around his wrists. "Did you get the note your brother left on the door?"

"Yeah, I got it." Butch put his hand in his pocket and felt for the crumpled paper, but didn't pull it out.

"He said he was going to have you hurt my wife."

Butch's eyes were flat, and he said nothing.

"Look, I'm sorry your brother died. But, there was nothing I could do. He'd lost so much blood he was basically gone before I even saw him."

Butch remained staring silently back.

Steve explored Butch's impassive face and eyes. He tried to sit up, but winced and fell back on the bed. "If you have to do anything, do it to me, but leave Heather alone. She's got nothing to do with this."

"How long ago did they leave?"

Steve looked at Butch in wonder. "Did you hear what I said? Leave her the hell alone." He paused and took a few deep breaths. "Please."

"How long ago did they leave?"

Steve rocked his head back and forth looking up at the ceiling. "They left about a half hour ago, I guess."

Butch nodded. "How long is it going to take them?"

"I have no idea. Where is your other brother, JP?"

Heather entered the room. She stopped short at the door, and the ice cubes in the tumbler clinked against the glass.

Butch turned his gaze out the window. "I think he's dead."

"Dead! What happened?"

Butch said nothing. Heather brought the glass of water to Steve and held his head as he drank. "A bear got him," she said quietly. "He was chasing me, and this bear and her cubs attacked him."

Steve stopped drinking, and water spilled down his chest."Oh my God! Where is he?"

Still no response from Butch.

"A helicopter came and flew off with him," Heather said. "Where are Mike and the other guy?"

Steve glanced up at Butch who looked back at him. "Jesse tied me up. Then he and Mike took off on the ATV to find a car," Steve said. "I'm so glad you're safe." He pulled Heather down, hugging her close to him.

Butch heard him whisper in her ear. He noticed her eyebrows shoot up and her eyes shift to him then quickly down.

"What did you say to her?" he said.

Steve released his wife and held her gaze without looking at Butch. "Nothing. I just told her I love her."

Butch's eyes narrowed, but he said no more. A wary silence moved into the room over the three like a heavy fog.

Twenty-six

Sergeant Colton Anderson scanned the steeply forested mountains below. They were flying over the northern quadrant of the search area. It was unlikely the escapees had made it out of the state on the highways. No sign from the Montana Highway Patrol, and neither the adjoining states' patrols or the border guards in Canada had reported the red Mustang. That meant the men were traveling the back roads or holed up somewhere in the mountains. It was up to him to find them. Somewhere down there. Like the proverbial needle in the proverbial freaking haystack.

The radio crackled in his ear. "Colton, do you read me?"

The pilot and he exchanged glances. It was the sheriff. "10-4, this is Colton. Go ahead, Sheriff."

"That bear attack victim you brought in? He's one of the Toomey brothers. Harlan's on his way to the clinic to get a positive ID."

Colton and the pilot both said "Whoa," and looked at each other with raised eyebrows. "Is he still alive?"

The sheriff sounded impatient. "Negative, he didn't make it. Listen, I want you to do a careful fly-by of where you found him. There's not much up that way, so keep your eyes peeled and see if you can locate the others. They may have stashed their car and be on foot, or hiding out in any buildings that might be up that way."

The pilot was already banking sharply to the north when Anderson responded. "Right, Sheriff. We're on it."

Annie pulled out of the clinic parking lot and, as was her habit, glanced down at the gas gauge. "Damn it!" She pounded her fist on the steering wheel. She'd never make it to the inn on less than a quarter tank. She made a sharp U-turn, and the tires squealed as she sped down Main Street toward the Gas-N-Go. Main Street was only four blocks long in its entirety, and she floored the gas pedal, zipping past the market, the post office, the hardware store and the two run-down saloons.

Her heart sank as the siren of the sheriff's car whoop-whooped from far behind her. The blue light flashed in her rearview mirror as it charged toward her from the other end of town. She checked her speedometer. Fifty. Twice the speed limit.

Shit! Not now, she thought and pulled to the side of the road. *I don't have time for this.* She ripped open the glove compartment and pawed through the mess of papers, receipts and makeup, knocking them onto the floor until she came across her registration and insurance card. She sat back and chewed on her thumbnail and watched in the mirror as the prowl car bore down on her. A block away it careened round the corner of Second Street and disappeared along with its siren between the houses, apparently on a different mission.

She let out a sigh of relief and pulled back on to the pavement doing her best to keep her speed under thirty miles an hour.

I should have told the sheriff to check the inn. Please don't let anything happen to Mike.

Her tires squealed as she turned, and the van bumped up the driveway to the Gas-N-Go. She pulled up next to one of the vacant pumps. It wasn't until she got out of the van that she saw the yellow police tape around the front door. A dark rusty stain on the parking apron just outside the entrance reminded her that this was this morning's crime scene. *Closed. The only place in this one-horse town to get gas and it's closed.*

Her stomach knotted, she circled the van and tried the gas hose anyway. *Maybe they left the pumps on.* The metal trigger of the pump clicked uselessly each time she pulled it. She banged the hose handle back into its cradle and let out a whimper. *Now what?* There was no way she could make it back to Thief Creek with this little gas. *Think!*

Madison.

Annie jumped in the van, banging her knee on the door as she entered. *Damn it!* She yanked the wheel into a screeching half-turn and gunned the van back up Main. Disregarding the speed limit, she jammed the accelerator to the floor. As she neared Second Street, she heard the sheriff's car siren again. Just as she was about to make the turn onto Second, the white cruiser came barreling down the narrow street, all lights strobing and its siren screaming. Annie slammed on her brakes and swerved to the side of the road, barely avoiding a collision as the sheriff's car shot out of Second Street and cut west up Main. In the moment that he flashed by, she saw it was Harlan yelling into his microphone with an intent look on his face.

She raised her hand and desperately called, "Harlan" into the closed window, but his car had already disappeared up the street. Her shoulders and her hopes sagged. *God, I hope that moron is on his way to the inn.* She let out a deep sigh and headed up the street.

The clinic was a block up Second. Annie charged into the lot and ran to the door. It was locked, and the lights were off. She slapped repeatedly on the aluminum door frame, shaking the glass and called frantically for Madison. She searched the parking lot for Madison's car, but all the spots were empty.

Her mind raced, and she slumped to the stoop with her back against the door. She choked back the emotion in her throat. This was a time to think, not to cry. The tears came anyway.

Behind her, she heard a metallic click and felt the door give way.

"Ms. Preston?" Madison's sweet teen voice was like an angel calling from above her.

Annie stood and absently wiped a drop of moisture from her eye. She wanted to hug the girl. "Oh, Maddy. I thought you'd gone home."

"Not yet." The look of concern on her face embarrassed Annie. "Are you okay, Ms. Preston?"

Annie nodded.

"I was just locking up in the back. I locked the front door and turned off the lights like you told me. I only let Harlan in. He just left. He wanted me to show him the body of that man torn up by the bear."

"What did he say?"

"Not much really. He just looked over the body and checked for that tattoo, then ran out of here and took off in his car. I locked up as soon as he left. I also got hold of Doctor Haroldson, and he's arranging to have someone from the hospital in Whitefish come to pick up the man's body."

"Oh. That's good, honey. Good work." Although she kept her voice calm, Annie's insides twisted like a raging tornado.

Madison beamed back at her.

"But, where is your car?"

"Oh, I walked to work after school. I left the car at home. Why waste the gas, you know?"

Annie knew that Madison lived on a ranch a few miles out of town. It felt like a rock had dropped in the pit of her stomach. "How'd you get to school this morning?"

"I got a ride from a friend. She's going to pick me up after work. Why?"

Annie sighed and ran shaking fingers through her hair. *Don't cry. Don't cry.* "I wanted to borrow your car if you had gas in it. I don't have enough to make it back to the inn, and I'm worried sick about Mike. The Gas-N-Go is closed because of . . . the robbery, and the phone's not working. I'm afraid those men—"

Madison put a comforting hand on Annie's forearm. "Sure, you can borrow my car. It's got a full tank. Let me grab my purse and lock up. I'll call my friend and tell her not to come. You can drive me home and take my car. No problem. I'm sure everything will be okay.

Annie looked at the girl through misty eyes and gave in to the urge to hug her. "Thank you, sweetie," she said, giving Madison a motherly embrace.

Madison blushed and smiled, then turned and hurried back into the building to retrieve her things.

Annie checked her watch while she waited. The second hand seemed to be dragging through molasses slowly tick . . . tick . . . ticking the time away.

TWENTY-SEVEN

A sharp glint from something in the gully below attracted Sergeant Anderson's attention. "Hang on," he said and craned his neck around to see what they had just passed. A badly battered red car lay on its side far down a rocky gully.

The pilot hovered, then slowly descended while Anderson stayed focused on the red metal leaning against a cottonwood below them.

"Son of a . . . That's it. Land where you can."

The pilot circled until he found a level patch of ground, and dropped the chopper down while Anderson called the sheriff. "Jack, I think we've found the Mustang. We're landing now. Looks like it went off the road and rolled into a gully."

"Great! What's your twenty?" Anderson heard the excitement in Tate's voice. This was a big case for the Lame Elk sheriff and for him.

"We're just about 3 miles from the turnoff onto Thief Creek Road." He checked his GPS and gave the coordinates.

"What's it look like? Anyone alive in there?"

"Don't know yet. We're landing now. I'll get back to you."

"10-4. Good work, Colton. I'm on my way."

Anderson, too, felt an adrenalin rush. He pulled out his service revolver as the chopper nestled onto the ground a few yards from the overturned car.

Keeping his gun ready and ducking against the rotor wash, Anderson crossed quickly to the car. As the rotors slowed their whirl, he called out, "Sheriff's department. Don't move."

The only response was the soft breeze and the lonely cry of a red-tailed hawk circling high in the sky.

Anderson made his way cautiously around the front of the Mustang. The license plate told him this was the vehicle they'd been looking for. It had tumbled quite a distance and taken a beating. He anticipated there would be four dead bodies in the car.

The driver's door was open, and he peered in. The vehicle was empty. Blood covered the back seat. Large rust colored steaks showed where a body had been dragged across the seat and rested against the outside of the car.

Walking carefully, the deputy inspected the ground around the car. From the variety of tracks, four men had apparently dragged some sort of device toward the rock face and up to the road. He knelt at the boot tracks and insured there were four distinct patterns. He tilted the brim of his Stetson back and scratched his head in thought.

If one of the men lost so much blood, it isn't likely that he'll be walking with the same gait as the other three Toomeys, or that he'll be walking at all. The boot prints indicate that the men were walking on either side of the . . . what? Stretcher? So, who do the fourth set of tracks belong to?

"Colton," the pilot called. "It's the sheriff. Wants to know what you've found."

Anderson climbed back in the helicopter and adjusted his headset. "Anderson."

The sheriff's voice was hurried and impatient. "Colton, Harlan's confirmed the bear victim is definitely John Toomey. I'm heading to Thief Creek. What have you found out there?"

"Nobody in the vehicle. Lots of blood in the back seat. Are you sure there were only four people in the car? I'm not positive, but it appears there is a fifth set of tracks. Like someone else was with them."

There was a slight pause as the sheriff digested this information. "I need you back in the air asap. Make it fast. We can investigate the crash scene later. Get some tape around the scene, then search those mountains. Carefully. Every inch."

"Yes, sir. Will do. Over."

"I'm on my way. Keep me posted if you see anything."

"10-4." Anderson returned to the car with a camera and a roll of yellow crime scene tape. He snapped several pictures, then cordoned off the accident area.

The pilot revved the engine as he climbed back in and strapped on his seatbelt.

With a nod to the pilot, the deputy pointed to the north, and they lifted into the blue Montana sky. "Keep it low," he said. "It's going to be hard enough to see anything down there through these trees."

Anderson scanned the terrain. They were a couple hundred feet in the air when the pilot nudged him. He turned and looked in the direction the pilot pointed. Below, two men were next to an ATV. One was on the ground with the other standing over him. While he wanted to get up to the spot where they'd found John Toomey, he needed to see what was up with these two men. If nothing else, maybe they had witnessed something. He tapped the pilot on the shoulder and waved his thumb down indicating for him to land.

∾ ∾ ∾

In the distance, Mike heard the growing pulse of a helicopter. A glint from the sky stabbed his eyes. He shifted his attention from the muzzle of Jesse's gun to the approaching chopper. Jesse followed his gaze and quickly shoved the pistol back into his pants, covering it with his shirt. "Get up," he said. "Get over here. That's the damn sheriff."

Mike got on his feet and walked over to the four-wheeler.

"Give me your cap."

Mike handed Jesse his cap and watched him pull it down backwards to cover as much of his red hair as possible. Sand and small pebbles peppered them as the chopper landed. The piercing look in Jesse's eyes sent a chill down Mike's spine.

"You're going to tell them we broke down, and I'm working on the engine. Nothing more. Get rid of them. If you try any bullshit, I'll kill you and the sheriff. I mean it."

Mike had no doubt that he did.

Jesse bent over the engine. Mike shielded his eyes from the whirlwind of dust as the helicopter landed.

The chopper blades were still running when an officer jumped out and approached them with a wave. Mike's heart beat with the same throbbing rhythm and intensity as the rotors.

"Gentlemen," the officer greeted them and stood before Mike.

Jesse barely turned his head, nodded briefly and went back to tinkering with the engine.

"Having problems?"

Mike hoped the cop didn't notice the sweat trickling down his face, or worse, the pee stain on his pants. He managed a weak smile. "Uh, yeah. A little engine trouble. Did you come all the way out here to give us a hand?" He broadened his smile.

The officer didn't appear to be amused. He eyed Mike carefully. "Don't you own the Bed and Breakfast?"

"Yes, I do. I'm Mike Preston." He held out his hand, but the deputy merely nodded in return.

"Your wife works at the clinic, doesn't she? Annie?"

"That's right," said Mike. A trickle of sweat dribbled down his back. He felt like he had to pee again. "My guest and I were just out seeing the sights when my engine conked out. Fortunately, he knows more about motors than I do. He should have it started again soon."

The helicopter remained running in the background with a rhythmic cadence. Thrum . . . thrum . . . thrum.

The officer glanced briefly at Jesse's back then turned again to Mike. "Have you seen any strangers around today?"

Mike widened his eyes, nodded and shifted his gaze toward Jesse. "No, officer. Just the occasional deer and moose. You know. It's pretty quiet up here."

Mike saw the deputy's forehead furrow and his eyes narrow questioningly. The deputy glanced again at Jesse who had pulled a spark plug and appeared to be busy with it. He carefully unsnapped the leather safety strap on his holster, but then dropped his hand to his side. A glimmer of hope stirred in Mike.

The deputy paused, then turned back to Mike. "Uh-huh. There was a bad accident up the road from here. But, the car is empty. Nobody's been up to your place?"

"No, sir." *Maybe he was wrong. Maybe the cop hadn't picked up on his signals.* He tightened his lips and shifted his eyes once again to Jesse's back, but this time the officer didn't show any sign of noticing. Mike had a sinking feeling in the pit of his stomach.

"Okay, then." The deputy tugged the brim of his Stetson and turned. To Jesse's back, he said, "You want me to call someone to come up and help you out?"

Jesse cleared his throat and called over his shoulder, "That's okay. I got it. Thanks."

"All right, then," the officer said and turned. As he headed back to the chopper, the pilot gave the engine some fuel, and it whined as it revved. The faster the blades picked up, the deeper Mike's desperation grew. He wanted to scream out to the cop, but the scream was balled like a fist in his throat.

Halfway to the helicopter, the deputy suddenly turned and drew his revolver, aiming it with both hands at Jesse. "All right, Toomey, stand up slowly and—"

In a flash, Jesse drew his own gun, rolled and fired, hitting the officer in the face. Mike watched in disbelief as the deputy's head snapped back, his beige Stetson flew in the air, and he collapsed on the ground. At the same instant, he heard the helicopter engine rev, and the pilot yell into his mouthpiece. "Officer down! Officer down! Anderson's been . . . "

The engine whined in protest, and the giant blades picked up momentum. The skids of the chopper lifted off the ground, and Mike steeled himself against flying dirt and debris.

The chopper was no more than ten feet off the ground when he heard two more gunshots and looked with shock as the pilot was thrown sideways in the cockpit.

The chopper banked sharply to the right and came crashing down. The blade hit the road, and the fuselage flipped over and smashed like a boulder into the ground, instantly exploding into a huge fireball.

Mike shielded himself from both the heat and horror of the scene, stumbling backwards, pushed by an invisible force both within and outside him. Somewhere in a fog he heard scrambling up behind him. As he turned, he felt, rather than saw, a rock-like fist batter the side of his jaw, knocking him off balance and onto his knees.

With ironic amusement, he realized he was actually seeing stars like in a cartoon, or at least, tiny flashes of lights inside his head. It felt at first that his jaw was broken. He checked with his hand and gingerly touched the side of his face. Behind him, the heat of the burning helicopter scorched his back. Somewhere nearby he knew lay the body of the deputy, and a few feet from there the flaming cockpit cremated the pilot's body. He felt like he was in Hell. As his head cleared, and the sharp pain turned to an aching throb, he realized boots straddled him. He looked up into Jesse's angry face. He was still holding the pistol.

"You son of a bitch. You signaled that cop, didn't you? I'd kill you now, but I need you to get me back to the inn. Get up."

Mike struggled to his feet. The flaming helicopter roared and crackled behind him. Black clouds of acrid smoke stinking of burning rubber, plastic and fuel whipped around in heat waves, stinging his eyes and nostrils.

"How much further did you say it was to your neighbor's place?"

"I don't know—maybe another ten miles."

"Ten miles!" Jesse kicked a rock across the road, then looked in both directions. He cocked one leg up on the ATV and sunk his head on his arm, thinking. After a few moments, he turned back to Mike. "All right, we're heading back to the inn. Do you have a map back there?"

Mike nodded.

"I'll get my brothers, and we'll hike out of here. C'mon. Let's get going." He pushed Mike forwards then stopped. "Wait a minute." Jesse turned back and picked up the officer's handgun. He smirked and stuck it in his belt. "This will come in handy," he said returning to Mike. "Let's get going. And no more bullshit 'short cuts.' This road will take us back. Move it." He pushed Mike forward and tucked his own gun in the back of his pants.

Mike glanced over his shoulder at the deputy's body and the tangled metal mass of the burning copter. Then, he turned and looked up the road, thinking about what lay ahead. He felt empty. Helpless.

"I said move it. Now!"

TWENTY-EIGHT

Sheriff Tate had watched for ten miles the column of black smoke rising into the sky like a map marker. Like a desperate range rider spurring his horse trying to outrace a thunderstorm, Tate bent over the steering wheel urging his cruiser to get to the damn exit. The few cars that he flew by were just blurs of different colors. He came up on them so fast they barely had time to pull to the side of the road to let him pass.

The siren screamed its pulsating wail in time with the throbbing vein he felt in his neck and head. His jaw hurt from grinding his teeth. Anger, frustration and even a rare sentiment of sorrow churned and harassed every one of his internal organs. The cautionary words of his doctor after his last heart attack telling him he needed to slow down in his life whispered in the back of his brain. Every other fiber in his body, though, was hell-bent on getting to the scene of the crash and getting on with capturing those Toomey bastards. He prayed he'd get the opportunity to shoot the sonsabitches.

What he had looked forward to as a quick arrest that would get him some great publicity in every newspaper from Missoula to Billings, as well as some much needed excitement not generally available in Lame Elk, was turning into a disaster of huge dimensions.

Bad enough the Toomeys had killed old man Loomis this morning. But now, it was personal. That helicopter had been his pride and joy. How many sheriffs' departments in tiny Montana towns had their very own chopper? Probably none. His was a very generous gift bequeathed to the department by his old fishing partner, a wealthy rancher who had a boatload of money and no family to leave it to. The bequest even included enough to pay for the pilot and the fuel for as long as he'd be around. And now? Somewhere below that evil black cloud of smoke lay his precious bird, shattered and incinerating.

He had heard every horrifying moment over the radio, from the desperate "Officer down" call to the gunshots, to the pilot's scream, and finally, the gut-punching explosion before the signal cut out.

"Damn it!" Tate pounded the steering wheel. The chopper and the pilot gone, and Colton . . .

"Officer down! Anderson's been . . . " The panicked transmission echoed in his head. He'd tried not to think about it. Not believe it.

Colton Anderson, whom he'd hired as his deputy ten years ago. He would never show it, but he looked on Colton like a son. He'd watched the kid play baseball in high school and bounce around for the whole eight seconds on wild-eyed broncos in the Kalispell Rodeo. He was pleased when the lanky young cowboy had applied for the deputy position. The boy was ranch-strong, learned quickly and was dedicated to the job. He was the closest thing to family Tate had. Maybe if his wife hadn't left him twenty years ago, he would have had a son just like Colton.

But Jack Tate wasn't a sentimental man. No way. He treated Colton like any other officer. Showed no favoritism. Kept things strictly professional. By the book. He was sure the boy had no idea how much he meant to him.

But now . . .

The road before him blurred, and Tate wiped the dampness from his eyes.

"Bastards. Sonsabitches," he growled, but the words came out garbled due to the damned lump stuck in his throat. He tried to jam his foot down harder on the accelerator, but the pedal was smashed against the floor as it was.

The smoke cloud had dissipated as Tate slowed to make the turn onto the ranch road. Even at the slackened speed, the cruiser took the exit fishtailing and swerving on the gravel. He ground up the mountain, taking the switchbacks with little caution. His jaw set firmly.

He rounded a bend and felt a sudden cold feeling in the pit of his stomach. In the road ahead a fire engine, an ambulance and a state trooper's car were parked with their red and blue lights flashing idly. Men were going about their separate duties with no apparent hurry.

Firemen sprayed down the blackened husk of the helicopter. The twisted metal looked like the coyote-picked corpse of some huge beast. A few yards from the wreckage two stretchers rested on the ground, white sheets covering the men beneath them. His men. Colton.

He exited the cruiser and was hit with a choking reek of smoke and fuel that permeated the air, burning his nostrils and making his eyes water. Tate stood outside his car for a moment staring at the two stretchers. His feet were stuck in the gravel. He strode over to the nearest one and squatted next to the body. He hesitated a moment, and slowly reached out to the covering sheet. His veined old hand trembled slightly as he pulled back the shroud. The charred, fleshless skull of the helicopter pilot grinned back at him. Tate choked and stepped away, his stomach churning. He walked to the side of the road and vomited.

He wiped his mouth on his sleeve and crossed to the other stretcher. An EMT bent over the stretcher and finished wrapping gauze around the victim's head. Colton. Tate felt a sharp pinch in his heart. An electric shock shot painfully up his arm, and his knees buckled. He dropped his head and steadied himself with his hand on Colton's chest. His breath came in tight hitches, and he stumbled to one knee. Sweat rolled down his face, and he felt light-headed. *Not now, God. Let me get those sonsabitches first.* He paused a moment and willed the pain away. He closed his eyes and prayed, *Take care of this boy, Lord, if you're up there. He's a good man.* Head bowed, the sheriff removed his hat and ran his hand over his bristly crew cut.

"Is he . . . " he asked the second EMT who stood next to the him.

The young man nodded briefly and said, "He's all but dead. Shot in the head. Very weak vitals. He's not going to make it back to the hospital."

"But, he's not dead yet?" Tate gripped the EMT's shirt sleeve.

The EMT looked down at the sheriff's hand. "No, sir, but the other one is." He nodded at the second stretcher. "Pulled him out of the chopper. Not much left of him. I'm sorry, Sheriff, but we've got to get these guys loaded and get going." The man hesitated for a moment.

Tate looked at him then down at his arm and realized he was still holding on to the man's shirt. "Oh, of course. " He released the shirt, and the two EMT's went about sliding the two bodies into the ambulance and slammed the doors.

Tate remained on one knee and stared at the back of the ambulance as it pulled away.

A tall Montana State Trooper strode over from the charred helicopter and laid his big hand on the sheriff's shoulder. "Hey, Jack," his deep voice brought Tate out of his trance. "What a bunch of crap, huh? I'm sorry about your boys."

"Yeah," was all he could manage.

"Toomeys, huh?" the officer said.

Tate sniffed and cleared his throat. The constricting band squeezing his chest was still tight as a tourniquet, but he was damned if that was going to stop him. He labored to his feet and tugged his Stetson back on.

"You okay, Jack? You look kinda pale." the state trooper stood next to Tate, concern showing on his face.

"Yeah, I'm fine. Sonsabitches," Tate said through clenched teeth.

The trooper, Bill Tomlinson, held his angry gaze. "We'll get 'em, Jack. Take a look over here."

Tomlinson guided the sheriff toward a four-wheeler by the side of the road. Tate glanced over his shoulder at the disappearing ambulance.

"Tank's empty. I'd say the Toomeys were on the four-wheeler when it ran out of gas. Your boys probably spotted them from the air and came down to check them out. Your deputy's boot prints over here and then going back that way tell me he hopped out of the chopper and confronted the Toomeys here. Looks like he was headed back to the chopper when one of the Toomeys shot him. Dropped him with one shot. Head on."

Tomlinson raised his finger to his own forehead. A chill shivered through Tate's body.

"Judging from the crumpled skids on the chopper and the trajectory of the bullets we found on the pilot, I figure he had started to lift off when Toomey shot him and he crashed from a few feet up in the air."

"Officer down . . . ," then the explosion. The sickening radio message replayed again in Jack Tate's head.

"So, Colton . . . , my deputy, wasn't in the helicopter when it crashed?"

"Doesn't appear so. He was several feet away from the crash site, and his body isn't burned. The pilot, though . . . "

A tiny wave of relief washed over Tate. *At least he didn't burn.* "What else you got?"

There was still a look of critical appraisal in the trooper's eyes, but he continued, "Well, there's supposed to be four Toomeys, right?"

Tate gave a quick nod.

"Take a look at these tracks. Those there are from your deputy. There are only two other sets here, and they go off in that direction. Where are the other two Toomeys?"

Tate pushed the brim of his Stetson back and scratched the side of his head. "Well, one of them's back at the clinic in Lame Deer. Dead. Bear got him."

The trooper's eyes widened in surprise.

"Don't know where the third one is," the sheriff continued. "No other vehicle tracks?"

"Nope. This four-wheeler came down off the logging road up there. But there aren't any other fresh tracks. Looks like the two men headed back up the road a ways on foot, but I can't tell if they headed up the logging trail or along the road. Either way, it's rocky and hard to make out any prints."

Tate paced off the boot prints until they disappeared in the bed of loose rocks. When he came to the intersection of the logging road he stopped and squinted first up the rutted trail and then up the ranch road.

Tomlinson came up behind him and said, "What do you think?"

Tate shot a wad of spit into the dry dust at his feet. "I reckon I'll go up this road here. You want to take the logging road?"

"Sure, I'll go up that way, but we should wait for some backup. These guys are clearly dangerous. "

Tate snapped at him, "Backup? I'm not waiting for any damn backup. Colton was my backup. I'll show them dangerous."

The sheriff turned and strode to his cruiser. The door was still open. He reached across the front seat and drew out a shotgun. He pulled some shells from his holster and jammed them into the magazine tube, then dropped the gun onto the front seat. He slid behind the wheel and slammed the car door shut. Forgetting that he'd left the motor running, he angrily twisted the ignition key. The car responded with a complaining grinding shriek.

Tomlinson leaned down into Tate's window. "Okay, Jack. You go ahead. I'll finish up here and call in some backup. Then I'll head up the logging road. By the way, they may have your deputy's gun. We couldn't find it. You be careful. Give me a holler if you come across anything. I'll do the same."

Keeping his eyes focused ahead, Tate said, "Right," punched the gas pedal, and tore up the gravel road.

"Sonsabitches!"

TWENTY-NINE

The late afternoon sun burned hot in the cloudless sky. A fat bull snake roused itself from where it had been soaking up the heat, slithered across the dusty road and disappeared into the dry ditch under a yellow tumbleweed. From the top of the weathered telephone pole, a red-tailed hawk took a break from its search for gophers, tilted its head to one side and observed the two men trudging below him.

Mike's legs were tired, and his parched throat felt like sandpaper. As he and Jesse arrived at the inn's driveway, each shuffling step he took was like another step toward the inevitable end of a ship's plank.

The entire way back from the four-wheeler he had listened to Jesse hobbling behind him mumbling and arguing with himself about how hot it was, cursing his brothers, strategizing and rejecting his next moves. Working himself into an angry wasp nest of hatred.

Mike's hands balled into fists. He wanted to tell him to shut up. He wanted to tell him to just take his brothers and leave him and his guests alone. He wanted to turn and strangle him. Throttle him. Bash Jesse's head again and again into the hard ground until his skull burst like an overripe cantaloupe. And he would dance victorious over the battered corpse, laughing and howling to the sky above. His lips formed a small grin at the image.

"Jesse," a twisted voice called out from the doorway of the inn, breaking Mike's hazy reverie. Butch stepped out on the porch. A too-small Ohio State University T-shirt stretched uncomfortably over his big frame.

"Where's JP?" Jesse asked.

Butch stopped midway down the steps. "He's gone, Jesse."

The two dusty men both stopped in their tracks and stared at Butch.

"Gone?" said Jesse. "What do you mean he's gone?"

"Gone. He's dead. A bear attacked him up in the mountain. A helicopter came and flew him off. But I could see he was dead. At least, he looked that way. It was a sheriff's chopper. I couldn't get any closer."

"Jesus," said Mike. He looked from Butch to his brother.

Jesse stood still in the yard with his mouth hanging open. Speechless. His slack-jawed face a mixture of confusion and anger. He balled his fists and raised them above his head. "What the—," he started, then let out an anguished bellow and shook his clenched hands at the sky.

"You shouldn't have made him chase after the girl," Butch said.

Jesse glared at Butch. "So it's my fault? Is that what you're saying?" His face turned red, and he took a gimpy step toward his brother, his right hand balled and ready to strike a blow.

Butch straightened to his full height and spoke calmly but firmly. "I'm just saying, JP wouldn't be dead if he hadn't been running after that woman. You should have left her alone, Jesse."

The two brothers faced each other like two gunfighters ready to draw, the one fuming, his nostrils flaring as he breathed in and out. The other stood ready and confident, imposing and unafraid.

After a few moments of the stare-down Jesse's shoulders relaxed. Butch walked over and put his arm around his shoulder. His brother slumped against him. "We need to go now," Butch said quietly.

Jesse stiffened and pushed his brother away. "I know that," he said. "That's what I came back to do—get you and JP and get the hell out of here. The sheriff knows we're in the area and they'll be here before long. But first, we've got to . . . Where's the woman? Did you find her?"

Butch looked down and scuffed his foot in the dirt. "Yeah, I found her. She's inside with the doc." He nodded his head toward the building.

Mike felt a pang of dread. Had Butch killed her like Jesse had Steve?

Jesse looked at the inn and back. "Did you . . . take care of her?"

Butch looked his brother in the eye and said, "No. No, I didn't do anything to her, Jesse. She didn't do anything wrong, and I . . . "

"Didn't do anything wrong? She about busted my leg, the bitch. Didn't you get my note?"

"Yeah, I got it. So what?"

Jesse stepped back as if pushed. Mike could see by the startled look in his eyes that he'd been taken aback by Butch's attitude.

"So what?" said Jesse, his face reddening. "So we can't leave her or these others alive, you big idiot."

Butch's eyes narrowed, and Mike noticed his lips tighten.

"Steve's not dead?" Mike blurted out. "I thought you shot him before we left."

Jesse smirked, "I didn't shoot him, I just wanted to get your attention." He pulled the pistol from his pants and pointed it at Mike. "Get me that map, Mike. Let's go."

The three men turned and headed to the steps of the bed and breakfast.

Mike reached for the screen door and heard the crunch of gravel from a car tearing up Thief Creek Road. All three men turned toward the driveway as the sheriff's white car hurtled around the corner in a cloud of dust. The cruiser skidded to a stop. Jesse stepped behind one of the porch columns and dropped to a defensive position with his gun pointed at the car. Mike charged inside the inn and flipped the latch on the screen door. Butch remained standing on the porch.

The car door opened and Mike saw the sheriff tumble out behind it, using the door for cover.

Jesse fired at the car and ducked behind the pillar. Butch remained still, as if in a daze.

A dark shadow emerged from the edge of the car door, and Mike realized it was the muzzle of a shotgun.

"Give it up, you sonsabitches," the sheriff yelled. "It's over."

"Jesse," said Butch. There was a resignation in Butch's voice that surprised Mike.

"Shut up," his brother snapped back from where he crouched behind the column.

The sheriff called out, "There's a trooper coming up behind me and more men on their way. You boys ain't getting out of here, so let's end it now."

"Jesse," Butch said. "He's right. It ain't going to do any good to keep fighting. We aren't going to get away. I'm tired of all this. Let's give it up."

Jesse looked in disbelief at his older brother. "You stupid son-of-a-bitch. You killed that old man at the store this morning. They'll fry you for that. Is that what you want?"

Butch stared at his brother for a moment, then spoke, his voice calm and quiet. "They kill us here or back in prison. Maybe I can get off for self-defense. I'd rather take my chances. I don't know what's best, but I know I'm done. I'm done, Jesse."

Jesse's eyes narrowed, and his jaw tightened.

"What's it going to be, boys?" the sheriff called.

Without unlocking his gaze on Butch, Jesse yelled back, "It appears my brother wants to surrender."

"Your brother's a smart man. Where is your other brother?"

"There's just Jesse and me, Sheriff," Butch answered. "JP got ate by a bear, and Tommy . . . Tommy's lying inside. Dead. The guy at the store this morning shot him."

There was a brief silence as the sheriff pondered this information. "I heard about the bear. How do I know it's just you two?"

From behind the screen door, Mike called out, "It's true, Sheriff. It's just these two. Tommy's dead."

"Who the hell are you?" the sheriff said.

"It's me, Mike Preston, Jack." Mike took a step outside the door and showed himself. The sheriff peered above the open door of his cruiser.

"Oh, okay. You all right, Mike?"

"Yeah, I'm okay."

"Anyone else inside there?

"Just my two guests," replied Mike. "And the kid's body," he added.

"All right," the sheriff called out. "Here's how it's going to happen. You're going to throw your guns out toward me. Then, you're going to come down here with your hands on your heads. I got a shotgun here, and I ain't too happy about what you men have done today. If you try anything at all that I don't like, I'll blast you straight to hell. Just give me a reason. Understood? Mike, you stay in the house."

Jesse stood up slowly and tossed the gun he was holding across the yard. "There's my gun," he said.

"Now, you," the sheriff pointed at Butch with the muzzle of his shotgun while still kneeling behind the car door.

Butch raised his hands to his head and began to walk down the steps of the inn. "I don't have any guns."

"You come on down and drop to your knees over here," said the sheriff.

With his arms over his head, the tiny T-shirt Butch was wearing rode up and exposed his midriff. Mike could see the intricate tattoos on his lower torso and back.

The sheriff seemed to be watching the ones in front as the big man sauntered toward him.

Mike caught a slight movement from the corner of his eye. It was Jesse. From the back of his waistband Jesse sneaked his other pistol and in one swift motion, brought the gun up and fired at the sheriff's legs before Mike could yell out.

The sheriff howled in pain and anger. He emerged from behind the door, stood and fired the shotgun toward the porch. The explosion was deafening, and pieces of shot peppered the front of the inn. Mike ducked back and saw Butch stumble with a lurch, clutch his shoulder and drop to one knee.

The sheriff pumped the shotgun, raised it and fired again without aiming. Mike cringed at the loud blast and simultaneously heard another one come from Jesse's gun.

The sheriff clutched his chest and crashed back against the side of his car. His shotgun dropped in the dirt as Jack Tate pitched forward face down next to his gun.

Jesse chuckled, then called to his brother, "Butch, you okay?"

Butch removed his hand from his shoulder and inspected the small wound, then got to his feet. "Yeah, just took a piece of shot. Nothing much."

Mike stood frozen in horror staring at the sheriff's body. He glanced briefly at Jesse, then opened the door and started down the steps toward Tate.

"Keep the hell away from him," Jesse ordered. "He ain't getting up. Did you see that, Butch? Got him right in the heart." He drew a pack of Marlboro's from his shirt pocket, extracted a cigarette and lit it up.

Butch grunted his acknowledgment.

"You can't just leave him there," said Mike, his chest pounding.

Jesse blew the cigarette smoke out through his nose. "You're mistaken there, Mike." His sarcastic tone made Mike clench his fists. He wanted to leap on him and throttle him, but he didn't move. "I can and will leave him here. And so will you."

"You're a son of a bitch," Mike spat out.

Jesse turned with an evil leer. "Son of a bitch?" he laughed. "He's right about that, ain't he, Butch? Our mother was a bitch, and our daddy was meaner than a poked snake on a hot rock."

He snorted at his own joke as if it was the funniest thing he'd ever heard. His exaggerated laugh slowed to a chuckle, and he spat a wad of spit on the ground. "Yep, Mike, that's what I am. A stone cold son of a bitch. And you and your guests are about to find out just how cold I am."

Mike felt his blood turn to ice water and shivered despite the ninety degree weather.

"Nice of the sheriff to provide us with some transportation, wasn't it, Butch?"

Again, Butch merely responded with a grunt.

A mixture of fear and anger coursed through Mike's body. "So, go on," he said. "Take the car and get the hell out of here." The directness in his voice surprised even him, but it felt good.

Jesse raised his eyebrows in a mock look of surprise. He threw down his Marlboro, then crossed the yard, confronting Mike so close that he had to take a step back. Even so, he smelled the smoky stench of the man's breath. His eyes were the cold gray of a soulless man.

"A little harsh for an innkeeper, wasn't that? Now what kind of a guest would I be if I didn't say goodbye to the rest of your visitors and you properly? Let's go back inside and take care of business, shall we?" He gave Mike a push on his chest directing him to the inn's doorway. Mike felt a sudden swelling in his bladder.

Butch, still holding his shoulder, said, "Come on, Jesse. Let's get in the car and get out of here."

Jesse snapped his head toward Butch and narrowed his eyes. "You know we have to take care of these people, brother." He paused as if noticing Butch's attire for the first time. "And where the hell did you get that ridiculous T-shirt?"

The big man's face and neck flushed red. "Heather gave it to me. It's Steve's."

Jesse chuffed. "Wasn't that sweet of her? You two getting along nicely while I was gone, were you?" He turned from Mike and stepped in front of his brother. The tone of his voice turned from sarcastic to threatening. The muscles in his clenched jaw twitched. "I thought I told you to take care of her."

Butch held his stare for a moment but then dropped his eyes. "They ain't going to do anything." He looked back in Jesse's face. "Let's just get out of here. Now. Leave them alone."

Jesse cocked his head to one side and squinted with one eye at his brother. "Just what the hell has gotten into you? When I tell you something, I expect you to do it."

Butch's shoulders slumped. "Jesse, I . . . "

"Jesse, I . . . " Jesse mocked his brother's speech impediment. "You what? You want to just run away and let that bitch get off with busting my knee cap? You want to run away and let these people tell the cops about us? Be witnesses against us? Is that what you want? What the hell is the matter with you?" He shot a wad of spit in the dirt at Butch's foot. "You make me sick."

A tense silence settled over the yard. For a moment, Mike thought the two brothers might break into a fight, giving him the chance to make a run for it. His foot shifted, and gravel crunched under his boot, breaking the silence.

Jesse turned his dead eyes on him. "Let's go, Mike. In the house."

On his way back to the inn, Jesse stooped and picked up the pistol he thrown out on the ground and handed it to Butch. "Here," he said. "You'll need this."

Butch eyed the gun. "Where'd you get this one?"

Jesse grinned. "We had a little set-to with a sheriff's deputy down the road. I offed him and the pilot of that chopper you saw. Gun's his. You should have been there. You would have loved it."

Butch's brow knitted. "You killed another cop? Jesus, Jesse. Let's just get the hell out of here."

Jesse pushed the gun into Butch's hand. "Take the gun, and let's do this. Then we'll get on the road."

Butch hesitated, then wrapped his hand around the pistol grip and followed Jesse and Mike into the inn.

Thirty

"In there," Jesse said and shoved Mike toward the Bridger Room. Heather sat on the bed holding her husband. There was an intensity to the look in her eyes. Mike couldn't tell if it was fear or anger. Or both. Upon seeing him, the tension in her face lessened slightly. At the sight of both Heather and Steve, still alive, Mike let out a sigh of relief.

"Mike," Heather's voice quavered, "are you all right? What's happening?"

"I'm . . . " he started.

"He's fine. For now. Don't you worry your pretty little head, darlin'," Jesse said giving Mike another push toward the bed.

The muscles in Heather's face tightened, and her eyes flashed frigid hatred.

"I'm okay, Heather," said Mike trying to maintain a calming tone. "It's good to see you too."

"Yes, it is nice to see you again, Heather," Jesse said. "I never got to say goodbye before you ran out the door earlier. After you smashed my leg."

Heather's cheeks flushed red, and Mike could feel the tension between the two reaching a dangerous point. "Look," he said to Jesse, "you and Butch have a way to get out of here now. There's nothing we can do to hurt you at this point. We have no phone to call anyone. The sheriff said there were other officers on the way. You should just leave us alone and go."

"He's right, Jesse," Butch spoke up from the other side of the room. "Let's get out of here."

"Let's get out of here." Once again, Jesse mocked his brother's cleft lip speech. "When did you turn so soft? I'm the one who got kicked in the balls, not you. I told you to take care of her." He jabbed his chin toward Heather.

"Look at her," he said and turned toward Heather eyeing her from top to bottom. "She's gorgeous. Why would you pass up a piece of ass like that?"

Mike glanced at Butch and was surprised to see a glint of embarrassment, maybe regret, in his face.

"We'll be leaving soon," Jesse said. "First, though, I want you to re-tie Steve to the bed, Mike."

"That's not necessary. Like I said—" started Mike.

"Just do it," Jesse barked.

Mike glared at him for a moment, then went around the bed re-tying the strips of sheet to Steve's wrists and ankles. Heather watched his every move with a clenched jaw. As he secured the final strip to Steve's right arm, she vaulted from the bedside and stood inches from Jesse's smirking face.

"You bastard," she spat out. "Leave us alone."

Jesse trained his pistol on Steve and pulled back the hammer. "Keep your distance, sweetheart, or I'll blow hubbikins away right now in front of you."

She took a step back, but Mike could see her body twitched with focused tension like a mountain lion ready to pounce.

"That's better," Jesse said. "Now, Butch, tear up some more strips from that sheet and tie the innkeeper to that chair."

Mike glanced at Butch who still had a look of concern on his face.

"Jesse, this—" Butch began.

"DO IT!" Jesse bellowed, and everyone in the room recoiled.

Butch glared at his brother for a moment, then turned and ripped the sheet into strips. He walked Mike to the upholstered chair next to the bed and strapped him firmly in place.

"Hold her," Jesse ordered Butch. "And hold her good. Watch out for her. She's got some fast moves."

Butch hesitated. The blood pounded in Mike's head. He glanced at Steve who had turned pale. Weak as he was, he squirmed against the restraints.

Jesse glared at him. "Damn it, Butch. I'm not screwing around. Grab her and hold her."

Butch reluctantly crossed the room and wrapped his massive arms firmly around Heather's compact body.

Jesse crossed to Steve and checked the straps.

Mike noticed Butch whisper something into Heather's ear. He couldn't be sure, but he thought it was "I'm sorry."

"That's good," said Jesse after checking the restraints on both men.

"What about her?" Butch asked.

Jesse eyed Heather with a smirk. "Let's take her into the next room."

Heather's eyes opened wide in fear and darted from Jesse to Steve then Mike.

"Leave her alone," Steve's dry voice croaked. He struggled against his bindings, but he had little strength and soon became exhausted.

Mike, too, yanked against the strips holding him and yelled at the two brothers. "You bastards. Let her go. Tie her up like us and get out of here. You'll have plenty of time to escape."

Heather twisted against Butch's vise-like grip to no avail.

Butch held her tight and said to Jesse, "He's right. Let's strap her down on the other bed and get out of here."

Jesse stepped closer to Heather and ran his hand through her hair gently caressing her head. He leered lasciviously, his crooked lips connecting with the scar on his cheek made his grin appear to run the full length of his face. "Strap her down, huh? Leave her alone? Butchie, you don't want a piece of this fine woman?"

Holding her head between his hands, Jesse bent into her hair and inhaled deeply. "Mmm, she smells good too."

As he pulled away, Heather snapped her head into his face and sunk her teeth into his cheek.

"Damn it!" he yelled and yanked away. Blood ran down from the little semicircle her teeth had made. He swung his arm and slapped her hard across the face, then gingerly dabbed at his wounded cheek, inspecting the spots of blood on his fingertips.

"You think I'm going to leave this bitch alone after what she's done to me?" he glared at Butch.

"It ain't going to do any good to waste time here," said Butch, holding the struggling woman. "Let's tie her up and go."

"Let's tie her up and go," Jesse imitated his brother again, adding an effeminate tone to his mocking mimicry of Butch's hampered speech. The men glowered at each other like two feral cats squaring off.

"All right," Jesse said, taking a step back and dabbing once again at his wounded face. "Tie her down on that bed over there." He pointed to the other bed with his chin.

Butch easily lifted Heather and carried her to the adjacent bed. Jesse walked over to Steve and pointed the gun at him. "Now, Miss Heather, you let my brother strap you down like a good girl, or I'll blow your husband's head off. Butchie, tie her down spread-eagle. And strap her tight. I don't want her wriggling free."

As Butch followed his brother's instructions, Jesse tore two more strips from the sheet and tied them as gags around both Steve's and Mike's mouths. He tore an extra one and walked to the other bed where Butch was tying the last restraint on Heather's ankle.

"All right," said Butch, yanking the piece of cloth tightly into a knot. "Let's get out of here."

Heather's eyes burned with a mixture of seething anger and fear.

"This is your last chance, Butch," said Jesse. "She's all yours for the taking."

Both Steve and Mike twisted against their restraints, yelling muffled oaths under their gags. Heather remained stationary. Glaring.

"You touch me," she threatened in a low voice, "and I will kill you."

This elicited a hearty laugh from Jesse. "Hear that, Butch? She wants you." He wagged his pistol in the air, then teasingly drifted the torn piece of sheet gently back and forth across her face. "Let's see, I've got the gun, and you are strapped spreadeagled on the bed." He leaned close to her face. "And just how are you going to kill anybody, darlin?"

Heather turned directly into Jesse's face and spat in his eyes.

He lurched back, then slapped her. "Damn you," he yelled, wiping his face with the back of his hand. "I've had it with you."

He handed the pistol to Butch, "Here, take this," he ordered.

Butch hesitated. "Jesse . . . "

"TAKE IT!" he roared, shoving the pistol into his brother's hands.

Jesse turned and snapped the strip of torn sheet between his hands. Despite Heather twisting her head wildly from side to side, he managed to wrap the sheet around her mouth. He made a knot and pulled it tight. Her cheeks turned red where the cloth bit into them. The imprint of her lips shown behind the piece of sheet. Heather's chest heaved, and her nostrils flared as she drew in and out what air she could. Her eyes burned into his with loathing hatred.

"There," said Jesse." I don't think you're going to be hurting anyone. Besides, you might even like this." He grabbed the top of her T-shirt by the neck and with a mighty rip, tore it off her. Her eyes grew large, no longer with anger, but with fear. She tried to twist her body, but the restraints held fast.

"Wow," said Jesse, admiring her naked breasts. "Butchie," he called over his shoulder without taking his eyes off Heather. "Would you take a look at this? You've got one gorgeous wife, Steve. You sure you don't want some of this, Butch? Last chance, brother."

Heather twisted her head toward Mike and Steve pleading for help with her eyes. Both men wrenched against their bonds, cursing soundlessly behind their gags. Before she turned back, he had unfastened and pulled down her jeans and panties. She bucked and screamed. Even muffled, her desperate cries filled the room.

"Hey," said Jesse, "if you don't want some of this, I do." With his hungry eyes still trained on Heather, he slowly, tauntingly unbuckled his belt, easing the strap back from the prong which sprung forward once it released from the hole. He gradually slid the leather end from the D ring letting the belt hang loose.

"Step away, Jesse." Butch's voice was firm.

"What?" Jesse said and turned to see the gun in Butch's hand pointed at him. The leer on his face melted into an icy glare.

"That's enough, I said. Now step away and let's go."

"You pulling on me?" Jesse said.

"I'm just saying we need to go." There was a slight break in Butch's voice.

Jesse crossed the room and pressed his belly against the gun's barrel and stood nose to nose with his brother. "Are you pulling on me, you giant, ugly hare-lipped freak?"

"I'm just saying . . . " Jesse taunted him, exaggerating the speech impediment. At the same time, catching him off-guard, he grabbed the gun from Butch. With his other hand, he pushed his brother back and trained the gun on him. Butch stumbled a few steps with a look of surprise and disbelief.

Jesse kept the gun on his brother. "I've had it with you today. I don't know what's gotten into you, but I'm sick and tired of you disobeying me."

Butch's chest pushed against the already tight material of the T-shirt as his breathing became heavier. Mike watched a bloom of red creep up his neck and into his cheeks. The big man's hands balled into fists.

"I'm done obeying you," he said. "You're just like Pa, telling me what to do. Insulting me. Bullying everyone like you're the big boss man. Screw you, Jesse. I said let's go, so let's leave. Now."

Jesse squinted at Butch and folded his arms as he took in his speech. "Screw me, Butch? Screw me? If it wasn't for me, you split-faced moron, you'd be back in prison. If it wasn't for me, you wouldn't have gotten anywhere in your life. You can't think for yourself. Never could. You're a damn loser. You should be grateful I've watched out for your sorry ass all these years."

"If it wasn't for you, I never would have been in prison," Butch countered. "If it wasn't for you I might have done something different with my life. You and Pa, you are two of a kind. All the two of you did for me was mess me up."

The two men glared at each other without moving. Then Jesse chuffed and shook his head. He relaxed and placed the gun on the chair at the foot of the bed.

"Now, I'm going to teach this woman a lesson. If you don't want to join me, fine. Wait for me out in the car. Soon as I'm done, we'll go. Okay, big boy?" Without waiting for a reply, Jesse turned his back on his brother and moved toward Heather, unsnapping his jeans as he walked.

Mike shifted his gaze from Jesse to Butch, twisting and yanking at the straps that held him. He watched as Butch strode across the room, clamped his hand on Jesse's shoulder and pulled him back.

As if he had anticipated such an action, Jesse jammed his arm up, knocking Butch back and off balance. With another quick move, he tore his belt from its loops and slashed it down across Butch's shoulder. Butch stumbled in shock.

"Don't you ever lay a hand on me," Jesse said and savagely swung the belt again, the leather slapping his brother across the face.

Butch caught the belt as Jesse swung it backwards for another blow. With a yank, he pulled Jesse forward and smashed his fist into his face. Jesse fell backwards into the wooden chair, knocking the chair, himself and the gun to the floor.

To Mike, it looked like Butch's anger was pumping him even larger with each breath he took. He leapt across the room, landing on top of Jesse and the two wrestled on the floor, rolling and punching each other. From his captive chair, Mike only caught glimpses of the struggling couple as they pounded at each other at the foot of Heather's bed. He heard scrambling, boots clattering, curses, grunts and heavily landed thuds as the two brothers whaled away at each other.

Suddenly, a loud explosion rocked the room. One of the brothers had apparently gotten hold of the gun. One of them cried out, and Mike's heart raced as he craned his neck trying to see who had been shot. A beefy hand appeared on the edge at the bottom of Heather's bed, and Mike watched as Butch struggled to his feet. A hopeful wave of relief washed over Mike as he saw Butch was the apparent victor. Jesse would no longer be a threat. Mike found himself praying that Jesse was dead. Almost simultaneously, he felt guilty for wishing another man dead. But of the two, Butch seemed the least threatening, the most logical and eager to leave. With Jesse out of the way maybe they had a chance. Now maybe they would be safe.

Butch crouched at the foot of the bed, tried to stand but stumbled backwards and crashed to the floor. His hand was clamped to his thigh, and Mike saw blood run through his fingers. His face was white, and his eyes were clamped shut.

Then there was a grunt and a rustling noise from the foot of the bed. Mike's glimmer of hope melted into disappointment as he watched Jesse struggle to his feet, still holding the gun. He had taken a rough beating from his brother. His face was swollen, and blood ran down from a cut above his eye. He crouched as he stood, favoring his wounded leg even more than before.

"Damn you, Butch," he said. "Look what you made me do. You dumb son of a bitch. I ought to leave you here."

Butch opened his eyes and rocked back and forth holding his bleeding leg. "You shot me, you bastard."

Jesse scoffed and shook his head. "Quit blubbering. You're going to be all right. I just grazed you. You smashed my sore leg. Here." Jesse limped to the nightstand and picked up the bottle of whiskey and took a large swig. He then carried it over to where Butch sat on the floor.

He shoved Butch's hand away from his leg and ripped his pants where he was bleeding so as to examine the wound. After a quick look, he poured a healthy dose of alcohol over the hole in Butch's leg. Butch clenched his teeth and pounded his fist on the floor.

Jesse took another long pull on the bottle and handed the remainder to his brother. "Here, drink this and quit complaining. You're going to be all right." He tore a long strip from the already tattered sheet lying on the floor. He wrapped the makeshift bandage several times around Butch's leg, then yanked it into a tight knot, causing the wounded man to jerk back, gritting his teeth.

Jesse snatched the bottle out of Butch's hand and took another deep drink. then set the bottle down next to his brother.

"Now you just set there," Jesse said as he stood. "I'm going to take care of Heather here, and then we'll take off. And don't even think about making another move on me."

With that, he turned and limped to the side of Heather's bed. He stood above her, admiring her body with a leer. Mike watched in horror as Jesse slowly unzipped his jeans. Heather's eyes were as big as saucers, and the gag around her mouth rose and fell with her heavy intakes of breath. She twisted and yanked at her restraints, but they held tight.

"Take it easy, darlin," Jesse said as his pants dropped to the floor. "I ain't going to hurt you. I should, though, after what you did to me, but . . . " He reached down and played with a curl of her hair between his fingers. " . . . instead, I'm going to give you something to remember me by."

He kicked off his pants. A malevolent chuckle bubbled up from deep inside him and turned into a sardonic laugh. Heather's body heaved in quick rhythm with her frightened breathing. She arched and twisted, pulling on the strips of bed sheet till her wrists looked raw. Mike and Steve cried out with muffled screams as they watched helplessly from their captive spots.

Still laughing, Jesse slowly began to pull his underwear down inches at a time, One side, then the next. Taunting. "You don't need to be so twisty, there, darlin. Just relax. You're going to like this. Watch me now, Doc. You might learn something."

The noises coming from Steve now alternated from raging screams to choking sobs. His gag was soaked, and tears ran down his face in a flood. Mike himself began to weep and hung his head, not wanting to watch what defilement was about to take place.

From the corner of his eye, he saw Jesse bend down and pull his underpants off. It was more than he could bear, and he squeezed his eyes shut and turned his head. He tried to will his ears shut to block out any sounds, but it was no use. Steve's strangled oaths and wrenching sobs stabbed into his head and heart. Not a sound came from Heather. Mike 's body shivered uncontrollably, and his heart pumped in time with his sobbing breaths.

Suddenly, a heart-stopping, ear-shattering explosion filled the world around him, and he snapped his head up and looked across to Heather who was screaming hysterically, her eyes wild with shock. Lying across her half-nude body lay the torn remains of Jesse, his back a gory mass of bloody meat.

Mike's heart pounded harder, and his ears rang painfully. He turned to the doorway and broke down, alternately sobbing and laughing. There, in the open door, stood Annie, his wonderful, incredible wife. The double-barreled shotgun from the mantle in her arms, still held to her shoulder and aimed at the bed.

The couple's eyes met, and Mike's filled with tears. His body ached to run to her, hold her and never let go.

Thirty-One

Annie stood for a moment without putting the gun down. Her body shook slightly, and she released the air she had been holding in her lungs. She looked from Mike to Steve and back to the mess on the bed. Steve and Mike kept their gaze on her, but Heather was still violently twisting on the bed trying to get Jesse's body off her.

Annie set the shotgun against the wall and crossed to Heather's bed. Before untying the woman, she clutched Jesse by the shoulders and rolled him off the bed. Both Steve and Mike cried out from under their gags. She could hear Mike rocking his chair back and forth.

"Just a min . . . " she started to say when she heard the metallic click of the shotgun hammer being pulled back. She turned to see a giant of a man in a torn Ohio State T-shirt standing on one leg and holding the gun. He held his other leg at an angle. Blood dribbled steadily from a crimson soaked bandage and pooled at his feet.

"You killed my brother." It was a statement, not of anger, or accusatory, just a simple pronouncement. His speech was strange. Then she noticed he had a cleft palate. His face was pale. She assumed it was from the large amount of blood he had lost. His arms were covered with tattoos. Just above the one on his shoulder, there was another bleeding bullet hole. A less severe wound, but no doubt contributing to the pallidness of his face. Rivulets of perspiration ran down from his forehead. He winced as he took a step forward favoring his bloody leg. The movement caused a fresh spurt of blood. She saw the pain in his eyes, but something more was reflected there. Sadness. Deep sadness.

Annie stood to her full height in front of the man and showed no fear, though her heart was beating against her chest. She lifted her chin defiantly and said, "You need to let these people go."

Butch said nothing but stood staring dumbly around the room.

After a moment's hesitation, Annie turned, ignoring the wounded man and approached Heather's bed. She pulled the comforter over her body and began working the knots on the restraints loose. As she removed the gag from her face, Heather broke down. She reached up and pulled Annie into a tight hug sobbing against her shoulder.

"I . . . oh God . . . thank . . . " Heather blubbered.

"Shh," comforted Annie. "You're going to be all right." She sat on the bed and held Heather while she calmed down. She turned to the sound of the thud of the shotgun stock on the floor. Butch had set the gun down next to a chair and limped over to Mike.

Not letting go of Heather, Annie snapped, "Don't you touch him."

Butch ignored her and bent and untied Mike's gag and the other strips on his wrists and ankles. "I'm sorry, Mike," he mumbled. "I . . . we . . . Tommy . . . " He hung his head and shuffled over to Steve and freed him as well.

Mike stood and rubbed his wrists then hurried over beside his wife. "Honey, are you all right?" he asked. Holding her against his stomach, he kissed her gently over and over again on her head. "Thank God you got here when you did."

"I'm fine," she said, "I was just so worried about you. I saw the sheriff lying out front."

Mike nodded. "I know. Jesse killed him."

"Steve," Heather called. She pulled the sheet around her and slid out the other side of the bed, then hurried to her husband.

"No," said Annie. "He's not dead. He wasn't shot. He had a heart attack. He had a defibrillator in his car, and I was able to revive him. I left him resting in his car. He needs to get to a hospital, but I had to find you. When I came in, I heard those men wrestling on the floor and then a gunshot. That's when I got the shotgun from the fireplace and came in here. It's a good thing I didn't miss. I could only find one shell."

A low moan from behind them drew their attention. Near the door, Butch weaved on his feet. He let out a deep sound like a sigh, then crumpled to the floor in a heap.

"He needs help," Mike said. "The first aid kit's next to the bed over there. I'll get it."

Annie crossed the room, knelt next to Butch and began checking his wounds. Mike placed the first aid kit next to her and followed her instructions passing her gauze, tape and antiseptic. She cleaned and patched his shoulder wound, then unwrapped the blood-soaked strip of sheet from his leg. "He's lucky. The bullet passed through his leg without hitting any arteries. But he's lost a hell of a lot of blood."

Butch's breathing was coming fast, and he mumbled incoherently. Annie picked up his wrist and checked her watch. The pulse was not good. Annie's mind clicked into professional mode. "Hand me my stethoscope. And get me the blood pressure monitor from our bathroom. Quickly."

Mike fished through the first aid kit, handed her the stethoscope, then scrambled out of the room to get the monitor.

"How's he doing?" Steve was up on one elbow watching her from the bed.

Without looking up, Annie held the diaphragm against Butch's chest. The heartbeat thump-thumped rapidly. "Not good. I think he's in shock."

Steve said, "Mike said you're a nurse, right?"

"That's right." Annie looked up at him, and for the first time noticed the bandages on his chest. "Good lord, what happened to you?"

"A little misunderstanding between me and your patient there. He went a little crazy when I couldn't save his brother."

Annie gave him a confused look. "What do you mean you couldn't save his brother?"

"I'm a doctor. His brother was bleeding to death and was too far gone when they brought him here. I tried to save him, but it was useless. That big guy came at me. I panicked. We got in a tussle, and he cut me with my scalpel. I'm all right. Mike helped patch me up."

As Annie tried to process this news, Mike rushed into the room with the blood pressure monitor and handed it to her. With rapid precision, she wrapped the cuff around his arm, pumped the bulb and checked the meter. "Damn it. His pressure's way down. He needs blood, or he's not going to make it."

"You can transfuse him."

Annie looked at Steve like he was crazy. "How am I going to do that?"

"If one of us is his blood type, I have what we need in my bag upstairs. Mike, can you grab that out of my room? It's on the dresser."

Mike left the room again and returned moments later with Steve's medical bag and laid it next to him on the bed.

Steve dug in the bag, pulled out a small plastic case, and handed it to Annie. "Have you ever used one of these?" he asked. "It's a blood typing kit. Very easy."

Annie opened the case and examined the contents. "No, I've never used one, but it looks pretty simple."

"It is," said Steve. "Use the lancet and take a sample from his finger with one of those sticks. Then rub the stick on those spots on the card. Wait ten seconds and then compare the results to that chart in there."

Annie performed the procedure with no problem. "He's B-pos," she announced holding the card for Steve to see.

There was a moment of silence as the gravity of what they were about to do settled on Annie. Steve, too, seemed to be thinking over the procedure. He said, "It may not work. It might be too late. I've got the needles and everything we need, but it still could be risky."

Annie mulled this over. "I know."

"I'm B-positive too," said Mike. "You can use my blood. Let's hurry up."

"Mike . . . " started Annie. She felt a hitch in her throat. She loved her husband. He wasn't the most macho man in the world, but if someone needed him, he was always there, no matter what the cost to himself.

"What?" asked Mike. He removed his shirt. "Come on, let's do this."

Annie and Steve exchanged glances. "Have you drawn blood before?" he asked.

Annie rolled her eyes. "Only about a million times."

Steve smiled at her. "Good. If you check in that compartment there, you'll find everything you need."

Mike lay down on the bed and smiled up at his wife as she wrapped the rubber tourniquet around his arm.

Annie smiled back. Her eyes glistened, and he noticed the little crow's feet at the corners that he loved so much. It had been a long time since he'd seen that sweet look on her face.

"I love you," she murmured.

"I love you too, sweetheart. Now be gentle with that needle."

From the other bed, Steve and Heather, arms around each other, watched the ironically tender scene as the innkeeper's blood snaked through the tubing into the plastic bag Annie had rigged up next to the bed.

THIRTY-TWO

As he rounded the bend, State Trooper, Bill Tomlinson, slowly braked his cruiser. Sheriff Tate's car sat in the driveway of the Thief Creek Inn, its front door wide open and the strobe lights flashing back and forth. He glanced over at his partner, then shut off his car's engine. Tomlinson nodded silently to the other officer, and the two men cautiously emerged from the cruiser, revolvers in hand.

Keeping a healthy distance between themselves, the troopers approached the car from opposite sides. Tomlinson was the first to reach the cruiser. The front seat was empty. He peered into the back and caught his breath. The sheriff's dead body lay prone across the rear seat.

"Jesus," he swore quietly. He signaled his partner to his side, then opened the rear door.

Jack Tate lay with his hand across his chest, eyes closed. His face had lost its color. Tomlinson couldn't tell if he'd been shot, and reached in to move his hand.

"Howdy, Bill." Tate's raspy voice whispered. His one eye was open just a slit.

Tomlinson jerked back so fast that he banged his head on the top of the car and knocked into his deputy who had been leaning over his back.

His heart thumped against his chest. "Christ, Jack. Are you okay? You scared the hell out of me."

Tate forced a tiny smile on his pale lips. "Heart," he said and tapped his chest with one shaky finger.

Tomlinson turned to the other trooper. "Get an ambulance or a chopper up here. Hurry."

The deputy trotted back to his cruiser. Tomlinson turned back to the sheriff. "We'll get some help up here right away. Can you talk, Jack? What's going on? What's the situation?"

The sheriff kept his eyes closed. His voice was weak. "Colton?" he rasped.

"He's alive, Jack. I checked with the hospital on the way up here. They think he'll make it."

Tate's eyes squeezed tighter and a droplet of moisture leaked from one of them and dripped onto the car seat. He swallowed and drew in his breath."Toomeys, " he wheezed. "Got my gun. Inside." He raised a finger towards the inn. Tomlinson glanced up, then back. "Shots fired. Nothing for awhile. Careful. Innkeepers inside."

Tomlinson's lips tightened. He reached across and rested his hand on the sheriff's shoulder. "All right, Jack. Good work. We'll take care of it. You rest. We'll get you out of here soon as possible."

He backed out of the car. After explaining the situation to the deputy, the two men made their way stealthily toward the inn. Tomlinson waved his partner to go around the back. Gun drawn, he took the front entrance. Before entering, he listened for movement inside. Hearing none, he carefully opened the screen door and stepped into the hallway. Taking care not to make any noise, he slipped down the dark hallway to the first door on the right. The door was open. He held his breath and darted his head into the room. A body lay on the bed lying in a bath of bloody sheets. The hairs on his neck that were already at attention, stiffened more and his heart drummed its wary beat. A quick visual survey turned up no other inhabitants of the room. He backed out of the bedroom, and saw his partner making his way up from the opposite end of the hall.

Voices.

The two troopers froze where they stood. They moved quickly towards each other and positioned themselves on either side of the doorway to the next room from where the voices had come. Together, they pulled back the hammers on their service revolvers. With a nod, Tomlinson directed his deputy to stay low. He placed himself in front of the door, gripped his gun and bellowed, "POLICE! Don't move," and simultaneously kicked the door open.

Thirty-three

The bedroom door crashed open and banged against the wall. Heather screamed, and everyone else in the room jumped except for the two bodies on the floor. Mike's first thought was *my God, what is it now?!* It took a moment for his brain to register that the two men with guns pointed at him were cops.

"Nobody move," the taller trooper ordered. His voice was strange, commanding but with an undertone of confusion.

The one behind him muttered, "What the—?"

Mike surveyed the room from where he sat in the chair, trying to take the scene in with fresh eyes as the cops must see it. Jesse's dead body lay torn and bleeding next to one of the beds. Butch was lying on the floor like some felled, tattooed giant with a bag of blood running into his arm. Annie stood over him checking the blood flow. Heather sat on the other bed, naked with a sheet wrapped around her. Steve lay next to her, bare-chested with a crop of bandages sprouting across his torso. As for himself, Mike's sleeve was rolled up and he sported a bandage around his arm where Annie had taken the blood. A shotgun leaned against the chair and a pistol lay on the floor. It had to be quite a sight for these guys.

The taller officer's body relaxed and he straightened up, but kept his gun ready. "State police," he said. "What—"

"It's okay, officer," said Mike. He got up slowly. His head felt light, and his legs were a little unsteady. He put on his innkeeper's welcoming grin, held out his hand and said, "Let me explain . . . "

Mike walked with the EMTs as they carried Butch to the ambulance. Just before they slid him in next to the stretcher holding Sheriff Tate, Butch asked the EMTs to wait. He looked up at Mike with cloudy eyes and said, "I'm sorry for all this, man. Really sorry. To tell you the truth, I'm glad to be going back to the joint. I don't belong out here. I never did." He turned his head and fell silent for a moment. Then he looked at Mike again and said, "Thanks for the blood, and thanks for trying to help with Tommy. He didn't deserve this. He was a good kid. He didn't do nothing wrong. Can you tell that to the sheriff?"

Mike nodded. "I will."

He watched as they set Butch inside the ambulance and closed the doors. The state troopers walked back into the inn to join the crew of crime scene investigators who were meticulously photographing and collecting evidence in the Bridger Room.

Annie and Steve stood on the porch on either side of Heather with their arms around her waist as Mike came up the steps.

He smiled broadly and clapped his hands together. "Well, just another day at the Thief Creek Inn. Can I get anyone some coffee?"

About the Author

After a career of several years as a Boston publisher, Jeremy Soldevilla moved to Montana with his wife and dogs. He and his wife owned and operated a bed and breakfast in Bozeman, where between making beds and breakfasts, skiing and fishing, he began writing novels. *Thief Creek* is the first of those novels. Jeremy currently lives in Boston.

Books by
Jeremy Soldevilla

Thief Creek
Murder in the Mountains
Second Chances